AN EYE OPENER

OTHER SHORT STORIES

about an ordinary life.

Mariki Kriel

AN EYE OPENER

and

OTHER SHORT STORIES

about an ordinary life.

MARIKI KRIEL

"Life is a succession of lessons

which must be lived

to be understood."

Ralph Waldo Emerson.

Contents

Page

For all my fellow travellers
accompanying

me on this amazing

journey called life.

Your contributions helped to create

the person I am today.

An Eye Opener

The clanging sound of ankle chains alerts her to the sluggish procession approaching the "eyes'" waiting room. *What the heck! Could it be? Prisoners and guards visiting the hospital?* Were they there for the same reason as she was?

Instinctively, she wants to diminish herself, hoping that, as a white woman seated in a government hospital, she doesn't attract too much attention. Her fellow patients pretend not to notice, but the tinkling sound of chains and shuffling feet fills the hollows of the corridor. The cavalcade of prisoners and their guards take the open seats directly opposite her. It's hard not to notice the guns displayed on the hips of the three guards.

What could be the matter with their eyes? She wonders, perplexed. To get this far in the hospital's system, one must have a valid condition, or otherwise they would have been sent home or referred to a later appointment. She should be aware because she was an inpatient of this hospital only two weeks ago.

When two showy men dressed in dark suits arrive to sit next to the prisoners, she sits up straight. Like a true crime detective, she notices that, unlike the other patients, they don't have any documents or hospital correspondence in their hands. Their sunglasses and the thick chain around their necks makes her curious. Hopefully, she must wait a while before the doctor calls her for her post-operation check-up. This is going to be good entertainment.

So, this is what gangsters look like – exuding confidence and authority. Despite their bravado, a sense of criminality hangs around them. The obvious bulges in the front of their trousers implies hidden cachets of contraband. The shopping bags they carry surely don't contain gifts for Aunty Maria in Ward D7! She watched surreptitiously to see what kind of communication was going to transpire between the two men, the prisoners, and the guards. The other patients in the waiting area seem quiet and nervous, their gazes averted to the floor or the ceiling.

One of the men gets up and saunters to the men's restroom. He appears after a while, shaking dripping water from his hands. Now, his pants aren't bulging anymore. Within seconds, one of the prisoners persuade a guard to accompany him to the bathroom. They noisily shuffle away – the chains between his legs restricting his movements.

On their return to the waiting area, they pause in front of the two suited men. They exchange a few sentences before a wad of R100 notes appears, just to disappear into the hand of the prisoner. The handover is swift and done expertly. Her estimate is that it was around R4000. The guard pointedly looks away while the prisoner puts the wad inside his trouser pocket. Soon after, the other two prisoners are accompanied to the men's bathroom by their guards. The guards seem nervous and make it obvious that they're agitated about the lengthy visits to the ablutions.

Shortly, she too has an urge to visit the ladies' room. As she passes the men's bathroom, she sneaks a peek inside through the slightly ajar door. She notices a broken toilet paper holder lying on the windowsill. A seemingly innocuous 12-centimetre roll wrapped in cellophane catches her attention.

'Excuse me, please.' She steps back to allow the cleaner to enter the room. She watches as he removes the broken holder to chuck into a black garbage bag. As she reaches her seat in the waiting area, the doctor calls out her name.

*****

It's rare for her to leave her home so early, but today is an exception. Nicole, her daughter who is working as an intern at the hospital, warned her that if she wanted to see an ophthalmologist at the Tygerberg hospital today, she had to arrive before the rest of the Cape Flats residents. Nicole spent her "Zuma year" at the Tygerberg hospital. The experience made her street wise and familiar with the hospital procedures and systems. 'Mom, the earlier your name is registered for the day, the higher is the probability that you'll be seen by a doctor. Nevertheless, prepare yourself for a long wait.'

From previous experience, she knew that her case was urgent. A retinal detachment isn't something to postpone or "keep on the ice." One might permanently lose one's sight if you delay an examination by a doctor.

Yesterday, like a thief in the night, a black curtain obscured her sight. At first, it was merely a sensation, an awareness. Maybe it was just her overactive imagination? She stood in front of the bathroom mirror, covering her healthy eye with her left hand. When she looked straight ahead, she could only see the outline of her nose. Though she didn't want to alarm anybody, she already knew the outcome. To solve this problem, she might require surgery or hopefully, laser treatment. It had to take place before the affected blood vessels dies and she lost her sight permanently.

There wasn't much time to consider the "when" or "where". She didn't have many options because her finances were in dire straits, and she struggled to make ends meet. Her hospital plan won't cover the specialist fees, so she'll have to take the same route as 80 percent of the South African population. The closest public hospital was beckoning her.

*****

Her initial retinal detachment as a young, pregnant mother, felt surreal and unrealistic. 'This is often a hereditary issue. To fix it, we'll have to remove your eye and band it. This is a large detachment, and it's the only way to save your eye,' said her doctor in a matter-of-fact way.

'But, doctor, will I be able to play tennis again? How will I take care of my baby? You don't understand, doctor. I'm only 22 years old and you're telling me that my life will change forever. As if getting a baby isn't a big deal already. Will I be able to deliver normally?'

'Dear girl. Don't stress too much. This won't be the first time I perform this procedure. You'll be just fine. All I'm asking is that when you arrive at the hospital, you lie on your side until after the operation. In that way, the tear in the retina will stay in its place. I've already arranged for a bed for you. When you leave here, you should go directly to the hospital.'

'But Doctor, I'm not prepared. What about my pyjamas? I don't have anything with me, not even a toothbrush. Oh, my goodness, this is a shock.'

'I'll explain everything to your husband. Maybe he could go to a shop to buy you a few things. When he comes to visit you after the operation, he could bring you the necessary from your home. Your recovery in the hospital will take at least five days.'

*****

Her mind floods with images of that hospital stay – the bandages covering her eye like Captain Hook, and subsequently the awareness that she had lost a quarter of her vision. The birth of her daughter was carefully planned so that she didn't strain too hard, lest there be too much pressure in her eyes. It seems as if it was yesterday. Hasn't she had enough troubles in her life to handle yet another one?

There isn't time for the standard "why me?" pity party. It has been conveyed to her that her mother's side of the family had poor eyesight and difficulties with their eyes - it was a genetic problem. And now it has happened again. The big difference this time is that she doesn't have a supportive husband who could buy her new pyjamas at Woolworths. But isn't having an attentive daughter studying medicine at one of the best research hospitals in the country even better?

She's not sure what she expected. Did she think she would get preferential treatment because of her daughters' connections? Or maybe she wished doors would automatically open for her. At the least, she hoped to be treated with respect. How absurd; she needs to grow up.

In 1973, when she had her first retinal detachment, Tygerberg Hospital was brand new. It's a tertiary hospital located in Parow, Cape Town, and was officially opened in 1976. It's the largest hospital in the Western Cape and the second largest in South Africa. It acts as a teaching hospital in conjunction with the University of Stellenbosch. Its mission is to provide affordable, world class quality health care to public and private patients within available resources, as well as excellent educational and research opportunities. Its vision is to be the best academic hospital in Africa, recognised for its world class healthcare service locally, nationally, and internationally. Like most things in South Africa during that period, it was duplicated with separate wings for "Europeans" and "Coloureds." With enough funds to support research facilities, it became an institution from which worldwide breakthroughs in medicine were made.

Now, thirty years later, mainly due to a lack of funds, the grand old lady has become rundown. Though her daughter studies there, she has never pointed out the physical decline of the buildings; her concern is always about the people – the doctors, the nursing staff, the patients, and her fellow students. If Nicole could be positive about her time spent there, why should she bling an eye?

Walking next to her daughter along the stark corridors, she squints with her healthy eye at the linoleum peeling off the walls like unravelling tapestries. 'Why don't they fix these walls, Nicole?'

Nicole replies matter-of-factly. 'There aren't funds for decorating things like this, Mom.'

She chooses to disregard the absence of aesthetics. After all, she's here for her eyesight; why should she be concerned about mundane things? It will be best to resign herself completely to her lot. Even if she had to wait there all day, she wouldn't grumble or complain. Not wanting to be idle, she wants to read Jane Austen's Sense and Sensibilities, which is the only book that fits into her handbag.

There are only six patients before her when Nicole presents her reference letter to the clerk at admin. Without that, nobody would get any further than this station. The assistant behind the window requests her ID and reference letter, which she kept ready in her handbag. Shortly, she is handed a green hospital card and a file. Nicole is now satisfied that she'll find her way, and leaves her for the gynaecology department, where she's currently assigned.

When she reaches floor H7, she hands her file and green card to the assistant who promptly discards it into a box. 'Please take a seat and wait for your name to be called. Next!' He shouts. When she turns around, she is confronted by a sea of faces waiting on wooden benches. *This must be a mistake. Who are all these people? Surely, they must be ears, lungs, or maybe livers. There is no way they are all eyes.* She turns around facing the assistant behind the glass window. 'Excuse me. Where must I sit?'

'Over there, take any seat,' he says pointing in the general direction of the 150 seated people. *Where did they all come from? So much for arriving early!*

Today, she promises herself as she walks fearlessly towards the eyes, *I won't be discouraged or dismayed.* Right at the back of the room, a vacant seat appears miraculously. She takes her book out of her bag and realises that nothing will make any sense to her today. The book serves as a shield and a lookout post while she learns the system. What does it take to get from here to see a doctor?

Somebody calls out of few names. "Adam Fortuin, Lenie Jacobs, Margaret Booysens, Louis Blankenberg." People get up from their chairs and rush out of the room. The atmosphere changes. Children start moving around, newspaper pages are turned, and patients displaying stickers on their chests showing they travelled here from the Platteland pass sandwiches around.

She adjusts to the rhythm and patterns of the hospital. Everybody tenses up as soon as they hear its name calling time. By now, she gets to recognise a handful of the patients. There is the older lady with a "pearl eye", the slim mother with the little boy, "blue bandage", and others. She becomes hungry and eats her sandwich.

'Listen for your name. Maybe it will be called sometime this afternoon.' Everybody laughs when the daughter greets her elderly mother. 'I must leave now; wait here for me.'

The waiting patients have formed a sense of camaraderie. A hawker offers peanuts and packets of crushed crisps for one Rand apiece for sale. 'It's cheap! Says the lady from Piketberg. The wife of "Sunglasses" is growing very impatient and often one can hear one of her heavy sighs.

She notices many elderly people and strikes up a conversation with a woman who comes from a farm in Namakwaland. *Salt of the earth,* she thinks. They've raised and educated their children off the income of the farm, but now the younger generation isn't interested in the farm and have become townsfolk. What should the old couple now do with their farm?

Her eye hurts. It feels as if it is threatening to erupt from its socket. But still she's concerned that the doctor might tell her there is nothing wrong with her eye. Maybe she's neurotic and exaggerates her symptoms.

'Lynn Potgieter. Go to room 61.' Finally. She hurriedly puts Sense and Sensibilities into her bag. In her haste to get away, she nearly stumbles over Sunglasses' boot. He seems oblivious to his surroundings.

A sign on door number 61, reads in bold letters: Sifting. A smiling, friendly doctor calls out names, then reads the patients' referral letters, before sending them away again. Some eyes are sent home or told to come back next year. Most are told to wait in a different room where their eyes are tested.

When she explains to the doctor that she's had a previous retinal detachment and that other members of her family have also had similar experiences, he says, 'That is the answer I expected.' He sends her to the next station, where her eyes are tested. She marvels at the nurses' patience while testing so many illiterate eyes.

A lady wearing a short, tight skirt with matching stilettos walks past her. She wears a blonde wig, heavy make-up, and lots of costume jewellery. Her clothes and clear desire to be attractive doesn't conceal the fact that she's no longer a spring chicken (or maybe she's a man?) Lynn is struck by the irony when the woman walks past a Seventh-day Adventist lady wearing a blue dress and black stockings. She can't resist a giggle.

She's now officially a member of the "drops" group. 'This is to dilute your pupil so the doctor can view what's going on inside your eye,' the nurse explains. From previous experience, she knows that it will take several hours for her pupils to adjust and shrink back to normal again. The group consists of six patients. She notices two men with overnight bags. On their chests, they have stickers indicating that they're from Fraserburg. Their GP must've advised them they might have to stay at the hospital for surgery.

When Nicole visits her during her lunch break, she goes to speak to the consultant. After a few minutes, she returns to fetch Lynn. 'Come, Mom. The doctor will see you now.'

'You have a retinal detachment,' says the doctor. 'We'll have to operate on you tonight. Look here, let me draw a picture of what we're going to do. Here is the damage: After we sedated you, we'll make an incision in the sclera, mend the hole, and finally crio or freeze the affected area. The procedure, from start to finish, could take one and a half hours.' Lynn feels relieved. She may relax now that she knows she's in expert hands.

*****

She imagines a beautifully decorated hotel-hospital with a welcoming duvet on the bed, colour prints on the walls, a menu with mouth-watering dishes, and even a glass of wine. This is what she may have expected if she were still married, but many things have changed since her divorce. The truth about what was happening to her finally struck home. *I'm no longer a bystander; this is real, and it's happening to me. I'm about to be operated on in a dreaded public hospital.*

A small flicker of hope makes her smile when they walk in the direction of an empty two-bed ward. If only she could stay in a private ward, she'd be content. But, no, she's admitted to a six-bed ward where many eyes stare at her. She senses the interest and queries surrounding her presence. 'What's she doing here?'

She changes into her hospital nightgown after the nurse performed an ECG on her. Next to her bed lies a middle-aged woman whose boyfriend injured her eye with a broken beer bottle. Though she walks with her head held high, Lynn can sense her rejection and pain. A 91-year-old lady, lying opposite her is going to have a cataract operation tomorrow.

In the communal bathroom she notices that the bath isn't dirty but after many years of scrubbing, the enamel has worn away. *Who cares about the condition of the chipped washbasin and the worn bathroom floors? At least I have eyes to see.*

*****

Lots of laughter and giggling wake her up in time for her premed Valium. 'Aunty, why do you let your tits hang out like that?' The nurses giggle.

'What do you mean? Look, where the ties are.' The old lady points at the opening of the hospital gown, not realising that she has put it on back to front. The nurses help her change it around, but then she chirps back, 'But now everybody can see my bum!'

Lynn giggles and rolls back onto her side. She could have been affluent, but if she hadn't had this eye-opening experience, she would have been considerably poorer. Nicole told her that one hundred outpatients are treated daily at the Tygerberg ophthalmology department. Many miracles in the name of medicine have happened there. *Do we really need to be treated in luxurious private hospitals at such a high cost? Have the poor been left behind? Shouldn't the solid building be dressed up to become the respectable lady Tygerberg Hospital once was? How dare they say there isn't money to keep her going above-the-bread-line lifestyle?*

*****

A week after she was discharged from the hospital, she had to go for a follow up examination. Since she now was a hospital veteran, she approached the encounter with an entirely different mindset. The five hours her visit lasted seemed to fly by.

The doctor was just as friendly and relaxed as the day she first met him. *Should I tell him about the prisoners and the drug exchange I witnessed? Maybe, or maybe not.*

He tends to his post-operative patients while handing out tips to his medical students for their examination the following day. Finally, he sets up his instruments to examine her eye. His mobile phone rings, and he excuses himself.

'I'm sorry, Lynn,' says the doctor when he returns to the consulting room. That was my bank manager who called.

We were discussing my loan application to buy new furniture for the private surgery I plan to open next month. When you have your follow-up examination in two months, you should visit me in my new rooms.'

'Thank you very much, doctor. But you've got to be kidding. I'd feel like a traitor to all the other eyes. I couldn't possibly miss all of this.' She spreads her hands to encircle the entire hospital.

'Healing eyes is one thing; opening them is quite another. But I'd like to see your new rooms. It will be convenient to visit you there because it's only a twenty-minutes' trip from my house.

*****

The Matric Dance

This was so annoying. Not only because Charlie had the audacity to make this request, but because I was unsure if he was pulling my leg. I mean, really! How could he expect me to take his son and his girlfriend to their matric dance in Stellenbosch with my car?

I don't mind driving; in fact, I enjoy taking a spin with my beautiful, luxurious sports car. Never mind that I overheard my wife and her best friend gossiping the other night.

'I'm convinced it's the male menopause, Jenny,' said my wife. 'That car is so low; I can't get into the passenger's seat without kneeling first. Ha, ha,' I heard them laugh.

'Oh, dear. Fingers crossed; Ben doesn't succumb to the impulse to buy a sports car too,' said Jenny in her husky, deep voice.

I had to suppress the urge to walk over to the two women sitting on the patio sipping the cocktails I prepared for them ten minutes ago.

"Impulse"! My word. Jenny needn't worry. Ben wasn't going to buy another car. He loved the power driving his four-by-four truck. He simply isn't the flamboyant type. Maybe I shouldn't set her mind at ease. Let her worry about Ben and his dark, mysterious ways.

My wife might have a point. No, not about the male menopause. Well, maybe a little bit of that, too. But mostly about the lowness of the car. I had to lose a few kilogrammes to make my stomach squeeze in behind the steering wheel. Since I've visited the local gym more frequently, my knees are more supple, and I have no problem whatsoever getting into and out of my baby. You see, one could say the car is good for my health. Ha, ha.

Without question, the colour of the car is red. Maybe that's what irks my wife. She might think it's a bit too flamboyant for classy, well-to-do folks. I can't tell her that I find it a stimulating colour, urging me to show off a bit. The truth is, they're hardly going to sell cars like this if they are painted in a safe colour. Everything in our house is 'monochrome'. Beige, white, and brown. Beige, beige, beige. I'm sick of it. The lovely painting, I bought at the auction to display above the mantelpiece in the sitting room was banned to the untidy games room, which we rarely visit. The orange of the strelitzia and the bright red of the dahlias, faded in the harsh summer sunlight to become as boring and nondescript as all our other expensive furniture.

*****

It must be complicated if you don't own a car to take your son or daughter to a special occasion. When I went to the matric dance, I had to walk there with a limping Molly hanging onto my arm. When we arrived at the town hall, my shoes were covered in dust, and Molly's underarms were damp with perspiration. To be fair, everyone walked to the dance except Willie Basson, whose dad owned the co-op and was wealthy. They drove a Studebaker, and we pretended not to notice when they slowly drove past us as if it was a funeral procession.

What I couldn't understand was why my father wouldn't lend me his car. He must have been aware that my friends and I regularly "borrowed" his car when he went to the monthly church council meetings. Sure, we were lucky that nothing bad happened on our trips on the dirt roads. I still cringe after all these years when I think of the night when the stray donkey appeared out of nowhere in front of the car. It was touch-and-go or I overturned the car, and who knows, one of us could've been killed that night.

Molly and I also had a narrow escape during one of her driving lessons in our Volkswagen Beetle. I was so in love with her then that I would easily have lied on her behalf should the man who collided with our car had been injured or killed. It was impossible to see oncoming traffic as she edged through the opening in the hawthorn hedge. What a shock we had when first a man and then his bicycle flew across the car's bonnet. Badly shaken and covered in dust, he managed to get up from the dirt road. He seemed unhurt.

My poor Molly was trembling with shock. I offered the man two Rand, which was all the change I had in my pocket. I wondered if he noticed who drove the car. He wasn't happy with the amount and objected. 'Sir, I think a fall like this deserves at least ten Rand!'

'Maybe next time when you come hurtling down this road, you should look where you go and not ride so close to the hedge.' I admonished him before he straightened the damaged front wheel of his bicycle.

It was no surprise that Molly didn't want to practice driving for a few weeks after that embarrassing incident.

*****

It isn't my fault that Charlie is a painter and can't afford a car. Do I owe him anything because he didn't make it in life and I'm the executive director of Brink and Botha? The perks and pleasures coming with that position exceed the blood and toil needed to keep our clients happy, but I feel I deserve each one of them.

Of course, I could also paint our house, but lately Molly has been complaining a lot about my absence from home. It's better that we pay Charlie to paint the house, and in exchange I'll try to be more available. I understand her unhappiness, but I don't think she has any idea what my job entails. Nowadays, she hardly has time to listen to me. The committees she serves on and the charities she supports keep her very busy. The only time we have for a conversation is when we get ready for bed. Tonight, I'll tell her about Charlie's cheeky request.

I can imagine her telling her friends at the club that her Jetta Cabriolet wasn't good enough for our painter. Ha ha. I have good taste and realise my Mercedes 450 SL will make a great impression on most people.

When Charlie asked me his "little favour," I told him to take a hike. He stared at me and pushed his cap to the back of his head. Some blue spots on his dungarees, covered in white paint, showed what colour it was originally. His eyes didn't flicker, and I knew he didn't take my gruff reply seriously enough. 'Good night, Meneer. I'll see you tomorrow morning.'

*****

As true as bob, tonight he asked me again! What a cheek! Again, I told him to forget about it; he should get an Uber, and I might pay for it.

It was Molly who changed my mind. 'You know, Mark. If we had a son and for some weird reason, we didn't have two cars, I wonder what we would've done. I mean, one's son is one's son, and poor Charlie only wants to give him the best he can.'

'You're right, Molly. It's no mean feat that their son is going to matriculate soon. That boy is dedicated, and he's certainly heading somewhere in life.'

I did a quick mental check. Thursday night is my only free night. I usually play a quick game of golf after work, and then I spend a few hours with my buddies at the nineteenth hole. That's my ultimate relaxation when I'm able to wind down and forget about the day's troubles. There's nothing to compete with a cold, frothy glass of beer after exercise.

Despite realising that I would be free on the night of the dance, I'm reluctant to mention this to Charlie. He mustn't get the impression that I'm at his beck and call. After all, I'm his boss, and he shouldn't ever forget that. We do, however have some kind of understanding, and by merely saying nothing, Charlie is aware that I'll help him.

'Charlie. Make sure my car is spotless, inside, and outside.'

'The red one, Meneer? Yes, of course, Meneer. You won't recognise your car after Charlie has cleaned it.'

I watch as Charlie leaves our yard with a happy stride. Tonight, he'll gain stature in his family's eyes. The news that Meneer will drive his son and his girlfriend to the matric dance in his red sports car will make them all very happy.

*****

After Charlie cleaned his paintbrushes on Thursday afternoon, he disappeared to the storeroom. I put on my cashmere jumper and splashed some Hilfinger Cologne on my hands and face. If Charlie thought I was going to dress up for the occasion, he had to think again.

Charlie though was dressed in his Sunday suit. Is that my old tie adorning his neck; the one I bought in Italy many years ago and gifted Charlie when I cleared out my wardrobe a few months ago? I kissed my somewhat bemused wife on the cheek and wished her a good evening.

'I'll have supper when I get home. Please keep something for me. This might take a while. Bye, my dear. Let's hope I don't get ambushed in the township.'

As I open the driver's door, I notice Charlie intends to ride in the back of the car. 'No. No, Charlie. Please come sit in the front with me. A not-so-subtle whiff of Brut, mixed with the smell of tobacco, reaches my nostrils.

'Meneer, the good Lord will bless you for your kindness tonight.' Charlie's intention is to appease me, but his ill-chosen compliment irks me more than he could realise.

We drive to Kopstamp in silence. I realise it's probably the first time that Charlie has driven in a sports car. Despite that, I sense his pride and excitement as he tries to suppress his smile. I use the time to plan my meeting with the Cape Town City Council which is scheduled for early tomorrow morning. This is a serious but complicated issue. The squatters who started to build shacks near my friend John's house will be allowed to live there legally if we don't oppose it in court within two days.

*****

As we enter the settlement, spectators line both sides of the muddy, potholed road. I wasn't prepared for this welcome, but Charlie must've spread the word. I feel my throat constrict and my heart pound beneath my cashmere jumper.

'No, Charlie. This isn't safe. I won't drive here. Can't you fetch your son and his girlfriend and meet me here at the main road?' Why did they choose tonight to have a riot? For Pete's sake. I don't intend to be stoned tonight while doing my Christian duty.'

'No, Meneer. Relax. These people are all our friends and neighbours who have come to look at our car. They'll never lift a finger to harm you; Charlie won't allow that.' Only now, I hear the chanting and shouting voices. "Charlie! Charlie!" I glance at my passenger and notice that he waves at the spectators as if he were King Charles himself. Maybe I should also greet these friendly, enthusiastic people. It's difficult, though, to keep an eye on the potholes and the high middleman on the crude road. A sportscar isn't built for rural roads. No, it should whizz down tar roads skimming the edges of a coastal road where the ocean reflects in one's eyes.

Our car? Just because he washed and polished my car this afternoon doesn't give him the right to be possessive with my prized vehicle. I wish I never gave in and allowed this to go so far. So much for doing a charitable deed. What am I doing here?

'Stop! Wait here, Meneer.' I abruptly stop the car on the side of the road. Charlie opens the door and hops out of the seat, forgetting how close he was to the ground. He stumbles and graze his knees on the edge of the road. The crowd jeers him and swiftly cover the car like a wave from the ocean would cover a rock.

Damn, Charlie has abandoned me. I think he's disappeared into a shack. The excitement of the crowd makes me lose perspective. Certainly, I've been led into a trap, and I'm going to die here tonight. "Successful business leader brutally killed in Kopstamp township." That is what the headlines in the Burger will be. Molly will make sure that my funeral is huge news.

Thoughts of my practical, trustworthy wife make me want to reach out to her for help. She must call the police immediately. Just before I manage to dial her number, Charlie appears from nowhere and opens my car door. The crowd makes way for him.

'Come inside, Meneer. They're ready for us.' I crawl out of my seat and follow him meekly into the shack.

It takes a few moments for my eyes to adjust to the diminished light inside the room. Charlie urges me to sit on the straight back chair; the only one in the room. I notice six glasses of Coke and a cake cut into six rather huge slices on a table in the middle of the room. From high up on the wall, Charlie's forefather stares at me with blank disinterested eyes. He's dressed in a khaki uniform with a bandolier draped across his chest. I vaguely remember that Charlie told me long ago that his grandfather fought in the Boer War.

From a show cabinet, baby trinkets, pieces of inedible iced cake, an ostrich feather, and more yellowed pictures stare at me. Cushions embroidered with cross stitch make the room look homely. I notice more ostrich feathers in a vase. Did Charlie's father work on an ostrich farm in Oudtshoorn before they moved to the city? My mind goes blank – I have too much to take in. That smell. Is that from an open fire in the adjoining room?

'Come here, Manie. It's getting late. Meneer doesn't have all night to wait.' The young man who shyly enters the room wears a dark suit and an embroidered waistcoat. The corsage he carries is obviously meant for his beau. A man with a camera draped around his neck follows Manie into the room. If only Charlie had asked me, I would've brought my video camera to take proper memories.

Outside, the crowd cheers loudly, and it's obvious something is happening there. A knock on the door alerts them to the girl's arrival. She looks like a princess dressed in a shimmering, gold ballroom dress. Her dark hair is coiffed into a beautiful style and adorned with a decorated comb. Maybe they have never seen the girl dressed like this because they seem overawed. Nobody says a word – no compliments are given, no acknowledgements made by Charlie's tongue-tied family. She's indeed very pretty, and I suppress the urge to clap my hands in appreciation of her effort to look so gorgeous.

I peek through the window. The crowd outside was now even bigger. *Where do all these people come from? I hope they don't scratch my car. The sooner we leave here, the better.*

Hardly any words are spoken, but somehow, the photographer managed to make them stand next to each other to pose for pictures. Even "Meneer" is part of the ceremony. 'Here, Meneer. Have a piece of cake. Coke? Would you like to drink a glass?' This is a different Charlie from the man who works for me. *It's so true: never judge a book by its cover.*

Before we leave for Stellenbosch, I must smoke a cigarette. My hands are shaking while I light a Lexington. As the nicotine runs through my veins, I feel how I relax. If I had to be honest, this is a great experience. Isn't this how we should appreciate the small stuff?

*****

The crowd encourages the princess to get into the car. They cheer and shout her name. "Charlene! Charlene!" She sits next to me, the corsage now tied to her slender wrist. I marvel at her composure and stoicism. Manie quietly hands me a CD, which I understand to be his message to Charlene. There are many ways of speaking without words.

I realise we're slightly behind schedule, and I put my foot down on the accelerator. Charlie puts his hand familiarly on my shoulder. 'Go for it, Meneer. That's what I like about this car. When you call, it responds.'

*****

When we arrive at the town hall in Stellenbosch, we are slowed down significantly by many other cars on the same mission. I glance back at the mirror to catch a glimpse of Charlie's gleeful face. He has achieved his goal. His son and his beautiful girlfriend's arrival for their matric dance will be the talk of the town.

'We must be patient. There are ten cars ahead of us.' I watch as each car edge close to the curb in front of the hall. A man dressed in an evening suit and white gloves opens the car doors for each young couple. Only once they've disembarked, the driver slowly moves away. There are vintage cars, long, flashy cars, four-by-fours, minis, and even a Land Rover.

As the princess gets ready to exit "our" car, she flashes me a big smile. 'Thank you, Meneer. I'll never forget this drive.' I get a warm feeling around my chest, and I wipe my eyes with the back of my hand.

'It was a pleasure, my princess. Go now; be the belle of the ball. You arrived here in a coach; don't become a pumpkin now!'

Charlie gets out of the back of the car to join me in the front. As we drive away to the sound of the car radio playing "Save the last dance for me," I slap him on the back.

'Well done! Charlie, how will they get back home after the dance?' I surprised myself with my untypical concern.

'My brother will fetch them with his van, Meneer.' I remember that Charlie's brother owns a window cleaning company, and he drives a truck emblazoned with signage: "Sparkling glass by Sam."

'Excellent, Charlie. No worries about that, then. Let's go to the pub for a beer. I'll show you where Tollies is. That's where we usually went as students.'

'Thank you, Meneer. Yes, let's go. You are my hero. Come on. Drive faster! Show Charlie what this car can do.'

*****

Mandy and her Friends

Chapter 1

If it hadn't been for her, my life would have been quite different. It's a pity I was so naïve then. I should have recognised the signs and signals. They were there, all over the ether, but I was so blinded by love that I ignored the vixen girl's trickery and deception.

You might imagine she has great looks or an exceptional intellect. How else does she manage to lure people away from good folks – from common sense, good manners, a secure life, family, and friends? No, she's not attractive or pleasant, and when she leaves my love's company, a stink and awful stench permeates the room. One's mouth tastes bitter and she'll make you turn your head away in disgust.

Her claims are quite alluring: she promises that she'll fill emptiness, she claims to know how to polish rough edges – all one's quirkiness will disappear, and you'll exude confidence. One of her many lies is that she'll make you smile at the world while she'll take care of your future. Of course, all these claims are unproven and obvious lies. She's obviously the mother of all lies, but she easily manages to deceive you. A few minutes of sweet pleasure with her opens hidden sewers and will make you gag for hours on her stench.

*****

'Do you have money for me, my lady?' He wears his new black shirt, and he styled his hair into a "spiky" look. 'Our milk has run out, and we need bread. When I return, I'll make sandwiches to grill with the lamb chops. I'll go to the Kwik spar and should be back in twenty minutes. Maybe I should put petrol in the car while I'm out.'

My first instinct is fear. Is Mandy going to arrive unannounced again? She left us in peace for three whole days. If only she would leave for good. But I shouldn't even consider her as a threat. I must have faith that good things will continue to be good. Where has my trust gone? Didn't I pray and ask for protection from her deception and betrayal?

'Please take my credit card from my wallet. Don't be gone for too long. Should I start the fire in the meantime?' I shouldn't show him that I don't trust him yet. He mustn't know that I fear Mandy's deceit and that I suspect that she might be waiting for him at the shop. She lurks in alleyways; she hides in the shadows. Obviously, I don't have what it takes to compete with her, but I shouldn't let him know how much I dread her. No, I must appear confident and show him that I feel secure in our love.

'Yes. That will help a lot if you can start the fire. Why don't you pour a glass of Sauvignon Blanc while you are at it?

I feel the softness of his lips on mine as he gives me the perfunctory "good-bye" kiss. He smells of aftershave and Colgate toothpaste. My body trembles as I pull him tightly against my chest. What is going on in his mind? Is he missing Mandy? How could I compete with her when he has known her since he was a teenager? They have come a long way together and have shared many experiences. Even though she humiliates him and causes him grief, he shares his pain and secrets with her. She always comes when he needs or desires her. Why would he prioritise me, a newcomer in his life, over her, his confidante and bestie? That knowledge gives her

31

strength and power, while my love for him appears fruitless and unimportant. He adores her even though she drags him towards his demise.

Perhaps I should emulate her strategies; learn from her how to lure him. She doesn't come cheap; she is scarce, expensive, and forbidden. He hides Mandy from me, but I have caught glimpses of her, the back of her head, an elbow, and a petticoat peeking from beneath her party dress. In my heart of hearts, I know I can't compete with her: the pleasure I can scrape together to offer him can't match the formidable spectrum of fantasies that have their origin in ancient times and interest him so much.

'So, I'll start the fire and make a salad while you're gone. When you return, you can braai the meat. Oh, I'm looking forward to a nice evening with you. Go now; please drive safely.' I turn to go into the house so that he won't see that I'm choking up. Why tears threaten to run down my face, I don't know. I suppose my nerves are a bit fragile.

Relax. He'll be back soon. Of course, the temptation of Mandy will always exist, and she might be calling him, but I must live my life too, and distrusting someone and fearing a girl who appears in the form of a pill makes is nonsensical.

*****

It's a balmy evening. The neighbour's dog keeps me company while I sit on the lounger, listening to the crackling of the dry, burning logs. I feel how the first sips of the cold Sauvignon Blanc calm my tension. The radio plays Saturday evening music, and my feet tap to the rhythm. Life isn't only good but also full of promise. The kitten Raymond brought home two weeks ago wants to play with the dog but becomes fearful when he barks loudly, and he rushes back inside the cottage.

I add more logs on the fire. The wood seems to burn quickly. The salad is ready, and I put it in the fridge to keep it cold. Should I pour myself another glass of wine? I don't want to be ahead of Raymond, so I'll pace myself. It's still early. He should be home soon.

Mandy, Mandy, Mandy! Why are you in my thought so often? Why do I fear you? When will you get the message that I am now his preferred companion? I don't intend to steal his life from him and bless him with shame like you do. No, I can see his good qualities, and once he told me about his dismal childhood, I understood his frustrations and lack of opportunities. Together, we'll be strong, and I'll be there for him all the way. Not like you, Mandy, who leaves him after your abuse and then laughs at his shame while lies stumble out of his mouth.

Raymond hates you too, Mandy. Yes, he's confessed as much to me. Though you bewitched him with your false promises, he admits he's powerless against your wiles. It seems you haunt him and forces him to choose between what he wants to do and what he really can't manage. Shame on you, Mandy! You're not his saviour, and he will tell me all about you in due time.

*****

'Where are you now, Raymond? It's getting late and I'm hungry. Will you be home soon?' His mobile phone went directly to voicemail. I leave the message speaking in a low tone, trying to sound strong and in control.

I take the magazine I bought yesterday and listlessly page through it. Inside me a time bomb is ticking. Whatever I do to prevent an explosion, nothing can deter it – it will go off at a certain time. Don't ask me what timer it's set to or how it synchronises with my inner clock – it is what it is. And right now, I know that I've been waiting too long. Something has shifted. What was good an hour ago, is now turning into a dismal, wet feeling of disappointment and dissatisfaction. I've been let down once again.

Should I go to look for Raymond; maybe he has a problem and can't get hold of me? I look for my car keys and then I remember that he has taken the car. What if I take my bicycle and pretend to go for a ride? No, that won't look good if he sees me riding in the neighbourhood. What will I say? 'I've gone for a little ride at ten o'clock at night to check on you and see who you're hanging out with.' No. That will make me lose face and could be risky this time of the evening.

The fire dies a slow, painful death. What's the point of feeding it when I know there won't be a barbecue anymore. 'Damn you, Mandy! You've spoilt my evening once again. From experience I know that it won't be just for one day only. Once she has deceived him, she clings to him like a leech. Her foul breath lingers on his hair until his next shower. He'll pretend all is fine, but if I search his clothes for signs of their rendezvous, I'll know he brought her into our house by stealth.

He meets her secretly behind closed doors and in dark alleys – nobody is supposed to know. I can see in his eyes; in the way he walks and talks that he has been unfaithful to me and himself. Would he tell her the same lies I'm supposed to believe? To be able to spend time with her, he plans and schemes for hours. She's not satisfied with his promise of undying love, no, she wants to have everything. "More, more, more, till death do us part," is her nagging refrain.

The elaborate preparations he takes prior to their meeting seem so wasteful considering the aftermath. Does it please her to know that his accelerated heartbeat, his anticipation of their coming union, keeps him in perpetual ecstasy which he tries to hide from me?

******

I brush my teeth and clean my face. What's the point of waiting? I worry about dreadful things that could have happened, but my hands and feet are tied.

Maybe there was an accident? What if he's hurt and in hospital? What if he has been in a fight? What if he brings shame on us? What if the car gets damaged and I can't go to work on Monday?

The kitten rubs against my legs. 'You poor thing! Are you hungry? Sorry Paddy. I'm also waiting for the milk. I hate to admit it, but chances are good that I'll have to buy milk tomorrow morning. Fingers crossed, there will be money left on the bank card.' I take the cat into my arms and go to lie down on me bed. Thoughts of Mandy drive me wild, and I stay restless.

Mandy is aware of my and Raymond's love for each other and her jealousy of me is obvious. She would do anything to drive a wedge between us. The nights when we sleep peacefully in each other's arms, anger her. As I pull the duvet over my shaking body, I wonder how many of those nights are still left for us. *Are those nights enough to make us survive?* I wonder. *What am I clinging to, trying to prove that despite all the warnings, I didn't make a mistake? But how was I to know that Mandy was going to be a third party in a polygamous relationship? Now it's too* late *and the damage is done. How does one admit to making such a calamitous mistake?*

Maybe it will be better if I'm tougher. It freaks me out that she knows my weaknesses. When I gain territory, she attacks me from a distant corner like a tiger stalking its prey; from a position that I never anticipated. Her tactics change with the speed of lightning and when I'm caught unawares like tonight, she mocks me and laughs in my face. If only he would protect me against her wiles, but no, he always sides with her. It saddens me to admit it, but he teaches her how to taunt me.

'Please, Raymond. If you prefer Mandy above me, go to live with her. She's not welcome here. You'll have to choose; it's her or me.' Making threats like these only make him nervous and seem to drive him into her waiting arms. She then becomes cockier and taunts me relentlessly.

Maybe I should take a sleeping tablet. I can't sleep while I worry so much about the "what if's" happening between Raymond and Mandy. No, I should stay awake to be aware of his arrival. Keeping tabs on his comings and goings have become my obsession, my preoccupation. I need to know when he's safely in the house. I might go outside to the parking area to check on the car after his return to see that he hasn't scratched it or have been in an accident. No, I shouldn't fall asleep.

I want to cry when I picture them together. Is he kissing her sweet lips until they become bitter and unpalatable? Are they gossiping about me, the other woman? If she manages to persuade him to desert me permanently, it won't take long before she'll urge him to find another victim. It's part of her strategy to break up unions; she wants to be in the middle like the filling of a sandwich. I turn on my side and pull my knees up towards my body. My deep sigh makes Paddy scuttle off the bed.

Oh, she's so frustratingly clever! She lingers just long enough to make me believe she has left forever. And then, out of the blue she'll arrive all smiles and full of promises. And then, like a fly that leaves the wall milliseconds before you hit and its blood splatters on your face, Mandy flees and pretends not to be interested in Raymond's demise.

We would laugh, sing, play, hug, and kiss, cook together, share a bath, plan our future and just as a happy smile spread over my face, she blows a trumpet to announce her arrival. I'm ashamed to admit it but she often brings along uninvited guests. How is it possible that I allow this to happen?

This is the secret: Mandy keeps company with the lowest of the low and because Raymond adores her so much, he is comfortable in their appalling company. Her taste, her smell and her dramatic effect on his senses is often too harsh, so he needs to camouflage her potency. She has no dignity or class, but he won't recognise or admit it. Her irresistible magic forces him to act beyond respectability.

I lie on my back, grappling with negative thoughts. Contrary to my nature, I attack Raymond, Mandy, and her friends with imaginary weapons. Why am I still enduring this unsavoury behaviour?

What happens to the friendly, kind, articulate, gifted person when the troupe of bandits arrive? He changes after he's spent time with them – everybody becomes his "friend". There aren't any strangers in his world when he's intoxicated by their offerings.

Mandy's friends aren't as choosy as her. They're more available than her and much cheaper. Lately, they have been arriving here on their own, acting innocent. A "natural product with little addiction powers," says the paramedical. He tries his best to convince me that these fellows are nice and a great substitute for when Mandy acts distant.

'Have you noticed these guys are buddies with builders and labourers? They give them courage to work hard and to last a whole day doing physical labour.' Raymond tries to convince me of the merit of these scoundrels.

'I really don't care about the habits of builders and labourers, Raymond!' The backdoor slams shut behind me as I step outside to hang the laundry on the line.

Does jealousy make me nasty because he prefers their allure to mine? Who gives this weed the right to join our intimate conversations. Why are they eavesdropping and then treat our deep thoughts with such disregard? Gosh! How wicked!

When he tries to stay without his visitors for more than a few days, he becomes withdrawn, argumentative, and sulky. Then, his words become arrows directed at my Achilles heel. Like a fool I argue back – right is right and wrong is wrong, or what?

*****

'My lady! Wake up! Come on, look what I've brought you! It took hours to pick all these flowers. I filled up the whole bath. They're all for you. Get up. Come look.'

'Oh, Raymond. Leave me. I'm fast asleep.' I drag myself with difficulty from a disturbing dream where somebody pressed me against a wall and held a knife against my throat. In a way I'm glad he woke me. For a moment I thought he was the man in my dream, and I stare at him. Is Mandy here too? Where is the crowd of fools? Is it them that I smell? What does that look of a wild animal I notice in

Raymond's eyes mean? My heart is beating fast, and I feel cold panic descend upon me.

'Come, my lady. I didn't pick those flowers for nothing. I think you call them daisies.' Raymond has pulled back the duvet and is now forcing me out of bed.

I glance at the alarm clock next to my bed. What time is it now? I wonder.

'Raymond! Where have you been all night? It's already three o'clock.'

'Aren't you glad I picked all these lovely flowers for you? Look at these Christmas roses. Just look, my lady. But, if you don't appreciate what I've done for you, I'll never bring you any more flowers. Never, ever! Unthankful woman! Go to sleep. I've got company that will appreciate me.'

He disappears into his bedroom and slams the door and leaves me to contemplate a bath filled with heads of white, blue, and pink hydrangeas, bunches of white Shasta daisies, and pink, blue, and purple sweet peas.

What will I do with all these flowers? Where did he get it from? Whose garden was plundered? Did someone see my car? Is he in trouble? Did he bring milk?

As I turn around to go to my bed, I notice my bank card lying on the table. Paddy sits next to it, licking his paws to clean his face. Tomorrow we should have a talk, Raymond, and I.

A dark cloud spews stink vapours from underneath Raymond's bedroom door. Mandy's friends always stay longer than she does. Too posh to overstay her welcome, Mandy has already left to look for her next victim.

Like a rag doll who has no control over its body, I sink to the bathroom floor. My legs have no strength to carry me to my bed. The smell of sweet peas camouflages my despair and obliterates the reality of my precarious life. Tomorrow is another day, with or without Mandy and her friends.

*****

Mandy and her Friends

Chapter 2

'Did you read in the newspaper there is an airshow at Ysterplaat this Saturday? I would really like to go. Not only can one walk around and look at the aircraft, but if you're lucky, you could win a prize and get to ride in a helicopter. Of course, the highlight will be the display of military jets doing their feats. Wouldn't that be fun to watch, my lady? There will be food and vending machines, but no alcohol, which makes sense!'

'That's a cool idea. Of course, we should go. If we take a blanket, we can sit on the grass to watch the show. Maybe we can make sandwiches and take our own snacks. I imagine the entrance fee will take up most of our entertainment budget for the month.'

Raymond lost his job a week ago and is now unemployed. I suspect Mandy had something to do with his discharge from the jeweller, who kindly offered to teach him his craft to make jewellery. It's a shame because he's incredibly artistic and could have turned that opportunity into a career. We urgently need his monetary contribution, and I hope he finds a job soon.

Ysterplaat is a military air force base with hangers built in the 1920's, and they have an annual show open to the public in October each year. The name Ysterplaat means "Place of Iron." I have never been to see a show, but I recall as a child when we lived in Milnerton in the fifties how pilots "broke" the supersonic sound barrier, which hurt our ears terribly.

41

'I'll buy tickets at the mall tomorrow. I'm hoping for nice weather. It's often very windy there.'

'Thank you, my lady. I can hardly wait. What do you want to have for supper tonight?' Raymond loves cooking for me. He often spoils me with a bubble bath when I arrive home after work. Nobody has ever been so attentive to me. Some days, he even selects my clothes and helps me dress. I would do a lot to please him too, as he's my family now. We're supposed to make our own friends and build a life from scratch. It's harder for Raymond, as he often misses Mandy and her friends, but I refuse to associate with them.

'You think you are so special, Katrien. Just because you lived a privileged life, you don't have to act like a larney.' Raymond can be mean sometimes, and I try not to show my confusion. It's obviously a slang word, but I'm unfamiliar with it.

'What do you mean? What does that word mean? "larney." I've never heard anything like it before.'

'Because that's exactly what you are. Posh, upper-class, vein and conceited. You believe you're better than a tramp, who sleeps outside under a tree or a bridge. Look there. Do you notice that woman begging at the intersection?' Raymond is on a roll now, and I must take my eyes off the cars in front of me to look at the woman who holds a paper cup in her hand, urging drivers to hand her a few Rand or some coins. She wears sandals and torn jeans with a dirty t-shirt. Her curly hair is dirty and tangled. Previously, I wouldn't have taken any notice of her, but today I'm forced to see her as a person who probably didn't know where her next meal would come from. Or maybe she's saving up for a bottle of cheap wine? A car hoots behind me, but I must wait for Raymond to put fifty cents into her paper cup before I can drive. 'Thank you, Meneer. May the Lord bless you.'

He's certainly opened my eyes to the situation of those less fortunate, desperate people. It's difficult to comprehend growing up in an orphanage, knowing your parents aren't dead in a car accident but are still alive and well – they're simply not interested in you. It's also not easy, though, to have stepped away from my life as a property owner and one who rubs elbows with the "who's who" of my town, to be open to seeing the other side of the population's daily battle to survive in the city.

'You see what I mean, my lady? You can't picture yourself as that lady, can you? You are larney. I promise you! Ha ha. But, nevertheless, you are cool, and I love you.'

*****

Despite our eagerness to go on our adventure, we wait for the alarm to urge us to get out of bed. It's already warm. Table Mountain tells me that Van Donk is puffing smoke from his pipe, which, according to folklore, is a forerunner of a strong south-westerly breeze.

'Remember to bring a jacket,' I say to Raymond as he is packing our lunch in the tiny kitchen. 'The weather is unpredictable, and the clouds are billowing across Table Mountain.'

'Thanks for reminding me. I'm ready now. Shall we go? I expect to see a lot of cars on the road. I want to stop at the shop to buy cigarettes.'

'Sure. Have you left the window open for the cat? Who knows what time we'll return?'

Raymond insists on driving, and though I find it hard to hand over control, I don't object. When he returns to the car holding a packet of cigarettes in one hand, my gaze is drawn to the small packet he holds in the other hand. 'What's that?'

'Oh, this is Mokador. It's a coffee-flavoured liqueur with a higher alcohol content than usual. He takes a big swig. 'Would you like a sip, my lady?' He smiles broadly, but the steel grip of fear puts me in a fight or flight mode, and my lips refuse to respond. This doesn't bode well.

'Let me look at the bottle to read what it says. Are you aware that it contains 36% alcohol? Come on, Raymond. You can't drink and drive. I didn't realise you intended to drink on this outing.' I wanted to say something like, "I hope Mandy isn't joining us too," but decided against it to prevent conflict and an argument.

'I'll be fine. Don't worry. You can drive back.' Raymond puts the car in reverse while holding the bottle of Mokador in his hand.

*****

'You fool! Stay on your side of the road. Where did you learn to drive?' Raymond stares aggressively at the driver in front of us and gives him the middle finger. It's hard to comprehend how quickly the alcohol took effect on him. There's about a quarter of the bottle of Mokador left, and I was astonished to see how his behaviour changed within half an hour. What else did he take before we left home?

'Raymond.' I would like to go home, please. You're already inebriated, and I don't want to spend the day with you. Please give me the car keys.' He just parked the car in the allotted area at the Military Airfield. There are many people mingling, carrying cool bags, folding chairs, and picnic blankets. Planes are parked in a designated area, while food stalls dot the landscape. I hardly notice any of this. My heart is pounding, and I am on high alert.

What are you scared of Katrien? I ask myself. *How about, attracting attention, getting hurt, or being reminded of similar situations as a child, all of which the result will be embarrassment? Isn't that enough reason to be fearful?*

'What the heck, Katrien? Don't be silly. There's nothing the matter with me. Go ahead and be a wet blanket if you want to. I'm here to enjoy myself today.' Raymond kicks the driver's door and slams his hands against the car's window.

I notice others watching us, and I step away, wanting to detach myself from the drama that's unfolding like a pot of boiling porridge left on a heated plate. As it boils over, I can smell dread. This is my drama, and it upsets me to know I brought it upon myself.

I didn't have to worry about Raymond because he quickly fades into the crowd. *Oh, dear heavens, what shall I do? From here on, his behaviour will only get worse. My car is locked, and he has the key with him. I don't want to be near him, so forget about him helping me. There's nobody to call and ask for help, nor is there public transport to take to get home. Unless I get a lift, I'm doomed to walk home. I can't stay here all day, and I want to avoid my protagonist at all costs.*

It can't be that far to walk. Just take one step at a time. Adrenaline will give me extra energy. Although my shoes aren't precisely walking shoes, a few blisters have never killed a serious hiker. I buy a bottle of water at a small café and soon find myself on the national road's shoulder, heading towards Paarl. Cars and trucks speed by. I'm hoping someone will stop and offer me a ride, but I don't want to draw attention to myself. Shock keeps me going, but tears streak my make-up since awareness of my horrible situation is starting to sink in.

This cycle of disappointment, hope, disaster, bliss, pain, and happiness is nothing other than torture. It must come to an end. But how exactly? What will happen to Raymond if I call it a day? What will happen to me? I've never lived onmy own and I don't know if I would know how to do it.

As I pass the airport's high fence embracing the side of the N1, my feet start to hurt. I had forgotten how long it takes to walk. It's a slow process, especially on such a hot day. From here, I can see the Plattekloof hill. Durbanville is still far from there. At this pace, I'll be lucky to get home before dark. I turn to stare at Table Mountain for a moment. Nobody will believe me when I tell them what's happening in my life right now.

Planes fly by in close formation. Pink smoke billows from their engines. I hear a car slow down; gears shift and then someone pulls over to the side of the road. I walk hesitantly towards the car. Did it stop to assist me? It must look strange to see somebody walk on this road, especially a woman.

'We're on our way to Tygerberg Valley. Do you need a lift?' I want to hug the friendly man with the two young children. They move up to make room for me in the front. It must be obvious that I have been crying.

'Oh, I'm so lucky. Thank you for stopping. My feet are hurting, and I'm very thirsty.'

'Where are you walking from? What happened to you?' The little girls appear tired and uninterested in me. I have an urge to explain what happened to me and that my own car has been "hijacked". Words and tears paint a picture of a slightly hysterical woman.

'Shame. That sounds tough. I could drop you off at the police station if you want to file a report.' The man seems very concerned about my safety.

'Don't worry. I just want to get home and sleep about it. Fingers crossed that my car arrives back safely.'

*****

It's about six o'clock when I arrive at the complex. I spent a few hours at the office where I work before, I took on the final few miles.

To my surprise, my car is parked in its customary bay, albeit a bit skew. It looks undamaged. I feel weak and start to tremble violently. The moment of truth has arrived, and I'm not ready for that fire. I had hoped to arrive first – to be cool, calm, and collected – and now I must walk into the lion's den.

No, I'm not ready yet. The door is closed, and no sound escapes the small house. This is unusual. Is the door locked? I don't have a house key with me; it's on the car key. Maybe he's sleeping and won't even notice that I 've arrived. Will he be concerned about me? Did he drive past me and choose to ignore me? I try the lock and to my great relief, it's unlocked.

I go to sit by the swimming pool and put my feet in the cool water. Think. Decide. Cry later. Be strong now. I hate Mandy. Now I hate Mokador as well. How many more enemies other than Weed are there? I hate myself. *Stupid girl!*

I circle the home like a tiger stalking its prey. The window at the back is open. I move the curtain slightly to peek inside. Raymond is lying on the bed. He seems sound asleep, but knowing the power of Mandy, I suspect that he's knocked out and will remain that way the remainder of the evening. That means that it should be safe to enter my house.

My home, or what used to be my home. If one must stalk one's own home, it isn't a haven anymore. I take a deep breath and remove my sunglasses before I hesitantly open the door.

Tomorrow, I must reach out for help, and I need to prepare for that meeting. I badly need a shower and eat something before I go to bed. I should quickly turn out the lights so that if Raymond wakes up, he'll be confused and may respect my sleep. The last thing I need now is a confrontation. This is the end of our road, but I must arrive at the finishing line unscathed.

*****

No! No! No! How could it be? This must be a mistake. My brain refuses to process the magnitude of the destruction lying in front of me. My fear of meeting a demented, crazed, living person was valid, but facing the aftermath of an angry, destructive person's wrath is equally debilitating.

What should I do? Oh dear, what can I do? Somewhere in the depths of my mind, a sliver of practicality appears. I should find the car keys and leave the house immediately. Preserve everything as it is to prove the crime. *Yes, sure, but where would I go?*

'Go to the police. They'll take Raymond into custody, and then you can sleep safely in your broken house.' My practical side takes no nonsense.

No, I'm not ready for that. Yet. So, what now?

'Do an assessment. What do you think happened?'

I believe Raymond lost the plot when he returned home to discover me missing. He lost it so badly that he threw everything his hands could find onto the floor.

The noise of the carnage must have been horrendous. The carpet in the sitting room is covered with flowers, shards of glass, shattered ceramics, torn pictures, shredded books and photographs, soil from potted plants, cutlery, knives, upturned chairs, and cushions. Surely, the neighbours had to be wondering what happened there.

My knees wobble and I start to shake violently. I walk cautiously through glass shards to the fridge to get a glass of ice water. I pick up a dining room chair, turn it over, and sit down. Think. Observe. *Look, my girl. This is your life. It's obvious that it's broken. Now go ahead and repair it.*

*****

I take a black plastic bag from the cupboard beneath the kitchen sink. Start at the beginning. See what you can salvage. Each item in this small house has meaning. They are symbols of a past that was intensely meaningful. Most of that's broken now, and I mourn for it.

'How dare you, Raymond? I've opened my life and my future for you, but now that you've demonstrated that you don't deserve my kindness, my "love" for you is useless. Do you know what? I'm leaving you to cope with this mess. Let's see how you'll react when you wake up from your stupor.'

I put the black bag down on the floor. Cleaning the mess isn't part of my resolution. After taking a shower, I go to my room, lock the door, and get into bed.

Paddy appears from underneath the bed and snuck up behind my back. The poor cat must have had the fright of his life.

Grief over a broken home and a shattered dream overtakes me. The alarm is set for early tomorrow morning. I must make sure that I won't spend the day in this place of destruction.

Sleep Raymond. Stay in your dark oblivion for as long as you want.

*****

Mandy and her Friends

Chapter 3

It's the sadness that wakes me, not the golden slithers of hot sun peeking through the blinds or the constant sound of Paddy's gentle purring. As the awareness that a new dawn is breaking descends upon me, I open my eyes with difficulty. The result of all last night's wailing left me with thick, crusty eyelids. Fixing my looks will require a lot of effort. But I didn't have a lot of time to decide what to wear or eat for breakfast. It's imperative that I leave before Raymond wakes up. I don't want to witness his shock when he realises what he did yesterday.

I tread carefully trying to avoid the carnage. How sad! *Don't make a noise. Be careful not to step on the glass.* A picture that escaped from my childhood album stares intensely at me from the floor. It was taken on the day I was christened, and it's one of the few pictures I have where my father is portrayed as a family man with my brother standing next to the seated couple.

If my mother had to know what's happening in her daughter's life today, she'd be very sad. Like yesterday, I can hear her say: "You should find yourself a man with a suit, my child. Then he can look after you. It's not that I don't like Raymond. I'm very sorry to hear that he had such a hard childhood and grew up in an orphanage. But Katrien, it's not a good idea for you to take care of him."

'Oh, Mother! Men with suits don't love women the way they should. All they are interested in is work, golf, meetings, committees, and planning rugby expeditions. They think they do a woman a favour when they accompany her to a shop. Show me a man with a suit who'll pamper me like Raymond!' My mother has a point, though. A man with a suit will have money and maybe own a house and a nice car, which he'd like to share with a good woman.

I'll have to work very hard if I insisted on pulling Raymond out of Mandy's claws. Though we've been to a few Narcotics Anonymous meetings, and we usually left there with new hope and vision, I realised within a few days that I had more understanding and knowledge of the so-called "disease", than Raymond. He's still flapping around in the shallow water of addiction – just as clueless and stubborn as before we sat at the meeting piously and holy, listening to advice.

*****

Like an elastic, I stretched the day as far as I could. Eventually it snapped, and I must return to my devastation. Not knowing what to expect, I park the car in the parking bay and sit quietly for a few minutes. What will I find inside number 38? What should I expect? Eventually I lock the car and walk slowly towards the front door like a criminal, knowing his execution day is looming.

At least I have a strategy now. Driving around aimlessly has given me time to create a plan – an idea of how I should get out of this mess.

*****

'Hello, my lady. Where have you been all day? I've been waiting for you.' Raymond and the neighbour's dog are sitting on the lounger on the patio. It's a good thing he didn't break that too, as it is one of my favourite seats.

'Hi, Raymond. Let me first put down my bag, and then I'll join you. Would you like a cup of coffee?' I refuse to look into his brown, questioning eyes. *Stay calm. Be civil. You win more bees with honey.*

Being inside gives me time to make observations. The broken house has been fixed somewhat. A few forlorn sweet peas stare at me from a metal jug. The pot plant has been replanted, and a few measly apples are placed on a paper plate in the centre of the table. There are no signs of the framed pictures of my family or plates from my Delft collection. *Oh, what the heck? They were just reminders of the past. Memories that make it through turmoil are the ones that will last forever.*

I'm relieved to notice that Raymond must have spent time cleaning up his mess. Though I wonder what went through his mind when he realised what he had done, I refuse to ask him. Even if he tries to explain what happened, there is no excuse for the carnage he caused.

I hand Raymond a cup of coffee. 'I put sugar in for you. We need to talk, Raymond.'

Raymond takes the cup from me. He averts his eyes from mine, but before he does, I catch a glimpse of shame. He has feelings, after all. 'I know, Katrien. All I can say is that I'm very sorry about what happened. You shouldn't have stormed off, Katrien. Why did you leave me by myself at the air show? That really made me mad, Katrien. I know I shouldn't have bought the Mokador. Somehow, it always stirs a pot of lava inside me.'

'Stop right there, Raymond. I don't want to hear your lame excuses. This is what's going to happen. My nerves are shot. I can't handle you and your Mandy problems anymore. You should sort yourself out, and maybe then we can consider being friends. I'm going on a little trip tomorrow. I've already called my work to tell them I have personal problems and won't work this week. If you wish to stay here until I return, you can use the time to find other accommodation. But I expect you to have left by the time I return. Your behaviour is making me crazy, and I can't afford to lose my mind.'

'But Katrien! You can't do that! What am I supposed to do? Where must I go?' I think Raymond realises that I don't want to be called "my lady" anymore. He is in shock. Tears fill his eyes. *Am I too hard on him? Does he need more time to arrange his future?*

'I'm sorry, Raymond. Tomorrow morning, I'm leaving for Knysna. I'm taking my bicycle and a tent, and I'll look for camping places enroute.'

'Can I please accompany you? I promise I'm going to change. Just give me one more chance, Katrien. You won't regret it.' Raymond is standing on his knees in front of me; urging me to look into his eyes. 'Do you seriously want to throw away the one person who loves you more than anybody has ever loved you?'

'No. That isn't what I would like to do. But tell me, do you seriously expect me to stay with someone so volatile and unpredictable?'

'I swear, I'll change. Please, Katrien. I'm done with Mandy and everything.'

'Don't swear, Raymond. You know I don't like swearing. Let your "yes" be your "yes" and your "no" your "no". And please wipe your tears. I can't bear looking at you. Please excuse me, I need to pack now.'

*****

This time I drive. The car is full to the brim with camping gear, food, water bottles, a gas bottle, firewood, and cooking utensils. Raymond travels light. His clothes for the week fit into a duffel bag, while I had to squeeze my swimming costume, track suit, and shorts into a small suitcase. I tuck the bag with medication for my chest infection into a gap behind the driver's seat. Antibiotics taken twice a day are likely to cure me of a nasty cough.

'Hurry. If we leave now, we might reach Mossel Bay before dark. There's a nice camp site close to the beach, and if we like it there, we could stay for a few days.' I can feel my anxiety levels rise, and I hope I haven't made another bad decision. Why is it so hard to become independent and step away from all that's bad for me?

'Here I am, my lady. I've locked the door. Let's go. Mossel Bay, here we come!' I glance at Raymond as he closes the passenger's door. Never knowing whether he is sober, and never trusting my instincts, I observe his brown boots, blue jeans, pressed blue t-shirt and watch. Finally, I search his eyes. He puts his black satchel bag on the floor next to his feet and smiles at me, challenging me to comment.

'Okay, Raymond. I promise I won't mention this on our trip, but let's recap before we leave. Do you agree with me that this is your last and final chance to stay with me in a relationship? Will you stand by the pact we closed last night that you won't ever use substances again and that you are going to seek help after we return from our holiday? Do you realise that I desperately need this break and that I don't want any trouble?'

Raymond takes my hand in his, and like on hundreds of previous occasions, my heart melts. 'Of course, I understand. Don't worry, please. I can't wait to start my new life. You are worth it. How could I disappoint you again? Right, let's go!'

*****

When we finally arrive in the town, it's already dusk. I didn't have the inclination to search for the camping attendant and pitch our tent in the dark. We find a hotel off the main road that shows the signs of a bygone era and isn't too expensive. Tomorrow evening, we'll camp.

'Shall we buy take-away fish and chips, Raymond? I'm so tired after all the tension of the previous days. All this coughing is quite exhausting. Let's have an early night.'

'Are you sure this is what you want to do? I mean, isn't camping going to be too hard for you when you already feel ill? To tell you the truth, I'm not sure that I'm so keen anymore.'

'What do you mean, Raymond? Don't make me mad. Please, just shut up!'

*****

This is like travelling with a child. The whinging, the nagging, and the sulking are working on my nerves. I'm seeing another side of my companion, and doubts have set in whether it was a good idea to give in to Raymond's request to accompany me.

As we leave the built-up area, I try to be positive and make small talk. 'That was a nice breakfast, or what do you say? It should last us until dinner time. Shall we push ahead and go to Knysna?'

'I'm not sure, Katrien. Don't you think we should rather turn around and go home? I'm not sure how I'll cope in a tent. I've never done this before, you know.' I feel blood rise to my head. *Focus on the road, Katrien. Don't lose it now.*

'Absolutely not, Raymond! As I told you, I need a break, and it already cost money to drive here. If you want to go home, here is your chance. I'll let you off, and you can see how you get home again. What is your problem? Are you missing Mandy already? Are you going through withdrawals, or what?' I notice a place where I can park and seeing no traffic behind me in the rear-view mirror, I slow down to stop the car. I'll call it a bluff. Surely, he can't be that desperate. This trip away from our familiar surroundings will be good for him too.

'Okay, my lady. I will see you when I see you. Enjoy your holiday. Let me get my bag in the boot. Wait, I must get something at the back too.' To my utmost surprise, Raymond is preparing to leave me to proceed on my own for my holiday. *What's he thinking? This is crazy! I'm not going to give him any money. He'll have to take care of himself once he has arrived home. I suppose he has lots of experience of hitchhiking. I shouldn't worry about that. He isn't concerned about me at all.*

Raymond opens the car's back door and I hear a paper bag rustle. What's he getting there? As far as I remember it is only my antibiotics in that bag. Whatever, he won't be going far on his own. *We'll soon meet up again. Don't let him see any concern on my face.*

'Goodbye my lady. Do you have R50 for me to buy smokes? I'll see you next week when you return from your trip, alright? Here, give me a goodbye kiss.' Raymond leans into the window to give me a kiss. I rummage in my wallet to find R50. If that's all he needs, it's not too bad.

'Bye, Raymond. Travel safely. See you next week.' I'm in no rush. Surely, he'll regret this stupid idea of hiking back

57

home while he could have a few days' holiday on the Garden Route. This is a great opportunity to forget about Mandy and make me happy. Maybe I should give him a few minutes to gather himself before I drive off. He'll soon return to the car with his tail between his legs.

The clouds that have looked threatening since early this morning decided to open their sluices, and it worries me that he'll soon be drenched standing next to the highway waiting for a lift.

While keeping an eye on Raymond as he narrowly misses a truck with a trailer that drove too fast, I pretend to do something in the car. Before he even has time to position himself on the opposite side of the dual road, a car stops next to him. Without even glancing at me, he hops into the passenger side of the large, six-cylinder car. Rain splatters from the car, leaving a cloud of smoke behind. They drive off with a roar. They're heading south. At that speed and with so much power, they should be home soon.

I'm horrified. Really? This is crazy. Should I also turn the car around and go home? All my hope, my enthusiasm, and my dreams for the future evaporate. A cloud of sadness envelops me. There are some things in life where one can't cross the Rubicon without consequences.

My hands tremble as I put the car in first gear. I'm not going back. My nerves are shot, and I need to gather myself. Gosh. This isn't how I imagined my first holiday in years to be.

*****

It's hard to focus driving with so much rain and the wet road. I'm shaking so much that my foot won't stay still, and my speed control is affected. I worry that I might get a speeding fine in an area notorious for its strict application. That thought reminds me of my financial situation. This trip is already pushing me into my overdraft at the bank. Once I return home, I'll have to focus and work out a plan of action how to survive on my own.

Would Raymond realise that he has pushed my boundaries once and for all? Has he any idea that I'm finally done with him? I take a deep breath and wipe the tears from my face. When I stop at my camping spot, I must remember to take my antibiotics. That would be a huge mistake to miss a capsule when I must sleep outside in a tent, so close to nature. Though it's late spring, the nights are still cool, and I hope I won't get cold or sicker.

When I see the sign pointing towards Victoria Bay, I slow down significantly. I impulsively decide. This is how far I'll travel. I don't have strength for more than this. I can't see the point of driving further. Healing can happen anywhere, but being close to the ocean will enhance the process. Oh, gosh, I'm terrified. If ever I needed a rehabilitation centre, I have found one.

*****

It took much longer than it should have to pitch the two-man tent. I missed a helping hand and common sense. Blowing air into the mattress took most of my breath, and I started to feel dizzy.

Where are my antibiotics and cough syrup? I search behind the driver's seat where I put it this morning. I'm convinced I didn't forget it in the hotel. So, where is it now? Was that the reason why Raymond looked there before he took off? How sly! He took my medicine, so that I would come home sooner. Well, if that's what he hopes for, he'll be disappointed. I'm not budging; I'll stay here until I'm ready.

It's full moon, and my imagination run wild during the nights. *What if somebody watches me and plans to attack me? It's obvious that I'm camping on my own. What if someone steals my car while I'm sleeping or go for a walk? What if Raymond sets the house on fire? What if he sells everything I own to buy time with Mandy?*

It's imperative that I find out more about my competition. Who and what is Mandy? I read on the internet that its scientific name is Methaqualone. Sold under the brand names Quaalude and Sopor, among others, it is a hypnotic sedative and sold as a combination drug under the brand name Mandrax. It contains 250 mg of methaqualone and 25mg diphenhydramine in the same tablet. Mandrax is commonly smoked. The tablet is crushed, mixed with dagga, and smoked through a pipe or broken bottleneck known as a "white pipe." Mandrax can also be swallowed whole or injected. The effects of smoking Mandrax include a euphoric high followed by drowsiness, temporary unconsciousness, or passing out, with potential sedation lasting up to 5 hours. Mandrax is a small tablet, varying in colour, that is highly addictive. Mandrax slows down the central nervous system and has a sedative effect. Dependency symptoms include irritability, sleeplessness, delirium tremens, mania, and epileptiform attacks. Amongst the adolescent drug misusers, Mandrax is known as "mandies" or "randy mandies".

I lie on my back in the dark, listening to the night sounds. Waves break on the sand, sending the salty smell of the ocean to my blocked nostrils. It was touch-and-go or I burned the tent earlier tonight when my scarf caught on the gas fire. My camping days are over. Tomorrow, I'll go home, where my future is unsure and scary.

My speech will be short but direct. I practiced my words once more.

'Hi, Raymond. I want you to leave next week. I don't care where you go; it's your decision. I'll buy you a bus ticket and give you R2,500 in cash. Paddy is my cat and will stay with me. Once you've left, you are never to contact me again. There will be documents drawn up for you to sign. Let me know where you want to go. Good night. Sleep well.'

I smile. Yes, that speech will address all the issues except for one more thought that came to me before I turned on my side to be able to hear the ocean even better.

'Oh yes, please make sure you take everything pertaining to Mandy with you. I never want to see or hear anything about her again.'

*****

The Helper

This morning Thandi woke up before her mother. Even though it was only 5.30 in the morning, she had washed and dressed already. As she braided her hair, she gazed at her glossy face as it reflected in the tiny mirror her mother had nailed to the wall above the table. She inherited her mother's almond-shaped brown eyes.

She recently watched her mother's sisters shake their heads and show off their pearly whites and heard them say, 'doesn't she look just like her mama?' The mirror is too small to show her legs, but she knows they are long – not perfectly formed but not lacking shape – where it's attached to her backside, full of promise. Her tummy protrudes slightly, hinting at fertility.

She had to hurry today. There wasn't time to wish she were thin like Manzi. It reminds her that Mama left porridge for her breakfast in the black pot. 'You must eat, Thandi. Don't try to starve yourself. In our culture, we value strong women. If you are skinny and appear to be made entirely of sticks and bones, no man will even look at you.'

Her clothes lay on their bed. When Mama got paid last month, she went to Ackerman's and bought the blue knee-length pleated skirt and the white long-sleeved shirt. She was pleased with the flat black slip-ons she received as a birthday gift. She didn't need to peek into a mirror to know how she appeared. When she was alone at home, she tried on her new outfit. When she took the mirror off the wall, she would hold it this way and then that way until she could see every part of her outfit. Not quite sure if she liked what she saw, she resigned herself to the fact that her mother had chosen the outfit for her. *Mama knows best. She said I don't have taste yet. It will develop over time. One day, when I earn my own money, I can buy what I like.*

Many of her friends submitted employment applications to the shopping mall near the national road that would open in one month. Sipho was scheduled to receive forklift operator training, and Fortune was still awaiting word on her application for the cashier position at Edgars. The lady who came to their school to speak to them about their future careers told them not to view employment as a job but rather as a career. 'If you put your mind to it and work really hard, you can become an important person one day,' she remarked. And Thandi believed her. Didn't she arrive at the school driving her own car?

Her little sister murmured in her sleep; her plump arms fought to escape as the blankets that were encasing her turned into a battlefield. For a moment, Thandi wished it were her sleeping so innocently. She needed to awaken her mother before leaving. Mama showed her yesterday which taxi to board and where to get off at the hospital.

She bent down to shake her mother's shoulder. 'Wake up Mama. I'm leaving now.' Her mother's eyes opened immediately. 'Oh, my daughter! You look so beautiful in blue and white. I wish your father could see you now.'

Both Mama and Thandi knew that she should have been wearing a full nurse's uniform today. For the most part of his life, Papa had been dreaming about that. But that would mean she would have to go to Alice to study at a college, and that could never happen. Not with her father working at the mines in Welkom and Mama needing help to raise her younger brother and sister. The thought of leaving her family home made her tremble. *No, I'd rather stay here, where I'm safe.*

Their history teacher informed them of this at school. 'Dreams become reality. Observe our leaders. They had nothing but dreams. Of course, there was a cost involved. They broke the yokes on their necks so that all of you could have a future in our country. Never settle for the meagre resources your forefathers had to work with.'

Mama agreed. 'My child, you don't want to spend your entire life working in someone's kitchen like me. Mama pulled a face and shrugged her shoulders while wiping her hands on her apron. Thandi noticed how dry the skin on her hands were. 'Yes, I know, Mr. and Mrs. Pretorius are very good to me. When we ran into financial difficulties, they lent me money, and they even brought me along to their Port Alfred vacation property. What future would you have, my daughter, if you did domestic work? No, we raised you to become more. You need to do something that will draw attention to yourself. We want them to value you and even depend on you – not to excavate their gold, wash their dishes, or clean their homes.'

Thandi only pays attention with half an ear because she's heard this speech many times before. 'Have you noticed, Thandi, that when you play with your brother and sister, people smile at you? And when you help your aunt Elizabeth carry her firewood, she always looks deeply into your eyes? You have a unique gift, Thandi. You're a helper. Never forget, my darling, that the "Mother of all Helpers throughout the entire Eastern Cape" was your great-grandmother from my side of the family. When you were born, the midwife prophesied and said you received this gift from your ancestors.'

Thinking about her mother's passion for her life made Thandi feel nervous. She would much prefer wearing the red jeans she spotted in the store window yesterday. Instead, she had to make her way to the taxi rank and wait for the 12-seater cab, taxi number 7, which had "Bra Darky" emblazoned on the front and sides.

As she gently closed their front door, she observed their neighbour, Mr. Umfadi, locking his front door with a large key. Instead of retreating, she slowed down. Normally, she would've greeted him with a mumbled 'morning' and trotted off to the taxi rank. But today, she was aware that she had an obligation. The fact that she was dressed in a blue pleated skirt hanging over her knees and a new white button-down shirt has elevated her standing in the community. Everybody in their neighbourhood knew Mr. Umfadi was dying. He was so thin that he looked like a locust wearing boots and a hat. He stumbled along, holding onto a stick made from woodfrom a forest near Da Noon. It was clear that he was also on his way to the taxi rank and that he needed assistance. If she were to help him today, she might arrive late at the hospital, and she could jeopardise her future career.

Taxis seldom wait and Bra Darky is notorious for leaving you behind – breathless, sweaty, cursing. The evil wind, full of dust, sand, and empty plastic bags, blew their curses and rebukes away to the nearby ocean.

Twenty girls from their school submitted applications to work in healthcare at the General Hospital, but only thirteen of them were approved. She was one of the lucky ones. They were warned that the Committee would watch their every step, weigh them, turn them inside out, and discard them if they found them unsuitable. On her first day as an apprentice, being late would undoubtedly work against her. She wouldn't be too sad if she weighed too little. She would much rather help Mama at home.

Mr. Umfadi stopped in his tracks and leaned on his stick. His breath came out in short, hissing sounds. He was standing close enough to her to smell the mixture of tobacco and old perspiration. It made her feel nauseous. Though it was only 6.15 a.m., she noticed trickles of sweat running down his face. Mr. Umfadi took a dirty-looking handkerchief out of his pocket and wiped his face with a quick movement of his hand. 'Be kind, my child. Help the old man get to the taxi, Thandi, please.'

This simple request put her in a quandary. It was too late to pretend that she didn't see him or know him. She didn't stand much taller than a pile of firewood when he was still healthy and strong enough to work on the farm. He used to help her carry water from the single shared tap, which was standing in the courtyard like a beacon, about 300 metres from their house.

Her father always praised Mr. Umfadi as a decent person. She had assumed for him to be so sick now; he must have done something extremely horrible. *Would a good man do this to me, forcing me to help him when it was obvious that I also had to be on time for the taxi?*

'Mr. Umfadi. I wish I could help you, but I must be at the General Hospital by 7.30 a.m., or I risk my shot at a bright future. They warned me not to be late if I was going to work there as a health care worker. I don't want to disappoint my parents, Mr. Umfadi. You must understand, right?' She beseeched him.

She can see the pearly cataracts obscuring the old man's vision through the layers of skin draped around them like a lizard's. The old man stays unperturbed. 'Thandi, dear Thandi.

Relax. There's still plenty of time before Bra Darky arrives. Don't you realise God placed you on my path today? I, too, must be at the General Hospital at 7.30. If you help an old man today, the spirits will bless you.'

Being reminded of the spirits made her conscience jolt. One didn't mess with the spirits. Maybe if she carried his bag, he might move faster, and they could still be on time. She realises that if she abandoned her elderly, sick neighbour without assistance, she'd never hear the end of the story.

And, so they plodded along, side by side. She, the young black girl with hope for the future in her heart, and the sick old man who realised that this might be his final visit to the General. The medicine he needed to collect today wouldn't provide him with a cure or extend his life, but it should ease his misery and comfort him. He has said his "good-byes" and set free his dreams like unharnessed oxen. He has also abandoned his plough and allowed his seed to be carried away by the wind. He had given up the idea of future goals or dreams. He will be given a month's worth of grey tablets by the young doctor in the white coat at the General, and he will consume them with the regularity of a village drum's beat.

*****

He already knew how this day would go. Bra Darky will drop him off at the hospital opposite the trauma unit. It will take a very lengthy, uncomfortable, and slow walk from the entrance down the hallway to "Files". Once he has arrived there, he'll engage in the usual game of musical chairs. Move up one chair, move again, one chair up, closer to the window where the clerk will ask his name before he disappears into the hospital's paper tummy. He'll stand there, balancing on his healthy leg and his stick, until he hears his name called. 'Mr. William Umfadi? Here's your file. Please wait at reception.'

67

He would feel the weight of the medical phrases nestled between the covers as he held the priceless file under his arm: tuberculosis, diabetes, fractured ribs, appendicitis, and ringworm. And the final inscription reads "cancer of the lungs". The whole span of his life, from being a young boy growing up in the Transkei, where he herded his father's cows, to where he is today, living as a displaced man in a shack on the outskirts of the city, is noted according to his illnesses. Oh, he's so tired. He longs to return home.

Finally, back at reception, he would ease his tired body onto a plastic bucket seat amongst fifty other bodies. He had to first visit a doctor to obtain those miracle medications that relieved his agony. First come, first served. There is no special treatment or favours for a dying man. It doesn't matter if he arrived early; he always had to wait for most of the day. He doesn't read, and the TV was so small and placed high on a stand against a wall that he couldn't make much out of it.

He would observe the people, much like he had done when he was younger, and watched the cows graze. In the spacious hallway, doctors, nurses, and office personnel moved purposefully, almost in running motion, as if they were eager to leave for greener pastures. He recognised a handful of the other patients. Would Old Eagle be present today, hawk-like snout and all, cussing and cursing as usual? He would get teased by the aids, who would block the wheelchair even though he might lose his turn at the doctors if he didn't arrive in time. 'Go away, fuck off! Get out of my way!' He would say this to the amusement of the other waiting patients.

He has noticed that white people frequently congregate near the two open windows. Maybe he should feel sorry for them. They look so out of place. He was convinced they were obliged to be there because private hospitals are very expensive. Although he had just enough money to pay for his food and tobacco, he had a bed to sleep on, and he took pride in his clean and neat clothes. Even he occasionally wanted to cover his nose when foul aromas and smells permeated the air.

What would he experience today? These visits to the hospital were a high point in his pain-filled life, and today might be his last. Should he share his thoughts with the doctor? The previous time he was here, he noticed a woman whose agony was obvious. 'I fear that my appendix will rupture.' She sat bent over double in reception until he left the hospital at 5 o'clock with the grey tablets tucked into his pocket. Her spouse was smoking by the gate. 'It will be easier to get into this hospital if you arrive in an ambulance. Nobody will notice or care if you die at reception.' He heard the man mumble; wishing he could reach out to the man who felt his wife's pain.

He chuckled softly as he recalls the young mother who dashed out to the doctor, whose signature she required on her paperwork. 'Oh, doctor, I'm so glad you're here. Could you please sign these documents?' As a veteran of the General, he knew she'd have to sit in those uncomfortable seats until her name was called. Two hours later, she grabbed her son's hand and walked past the impassive patients, muttering, 'How much longer do I have to wait? This is completely absurd. Let's go home.'

*****

He was aware that he was slowing the young girl down, but he needed her assistance to get into the taxi. To give her due, she restrained herself and paced her steps to meet his laborious hobble. What exactly is this "Health Care Worker" thing all about? She had grown up before his eyes, and he had never seen her do much other than carry water from the tap in the square 300 metres from their shack. Will she be able to look into someone's eyes, see their anguish and discomfort, and then help them? What happened to the world as it once was? Her young, robust body appears mature enough to carry babies, make clay pots, build huts, and plant mealies.

'Mr. Umfadi, please, hurry! Speed up! The girl pleaded next to him; her face contorted with dread. Bra Darky's taxi had just arrived at the intersection opposite the bicycle shop. Nobody got off, but four passengers boarded the vehicle. The driver spotted the elderly man hobbling alongside the lovely young girl in the pleated blue skirt. They motioned with their hands that he should wait for them, but he was on a tight schedule and had a "never wait" policy that served him well.

'Is it my fault that you're late? Maybe you could start earlier next time.' He yelled at them. He flashed them a big white smile while he put the vehicle into first gear and skilfully, albeit recklessly, pushed in front of an oncoming white Mercedes.

'Do you see now, Mr. Umfadi? Now we must wait until the next taxi arrives, and I'll be late. If I miss this opportunity, Mama will never forgive me.'

*****

'You're late,' said the vulture unnecessarily. 'I'm very sorry, but…' Thandi would like to explain the reason for her lateness, but she's cut short by the matron. 'Go to Ward G1 and meet Sister Bothma there. She'll tell you what you need to do.

Thandi must pass through the open doors of the high-care unit to get to Ward G1. Patients lay on their beds, flanked by trellises like caged animals. Their eyes are closed, and plastic masks cover their faces, with pipes emerging to synchronise her heartbeat. She wasn't sure if the horror she was feeling was her own or the result of defenceless bodies reaching out to her in a mass assault, pleading with her to help them.

Her legs feel wobbly when she arrives at the nurses' station. She is prepared to apologise for her tardiness once more. Unaccustomed to the sight she just witnessed, her attempt at speaking was once again thwarted by what she saw. The nurses were oblivious to her presence. Standing in a circle, holding hands, she heard them pray. "Please, Lord Jesus, guide us and let us be your hands and feet today."

The same eyes that had just been closed in prayer opened and stared at Thandi with hostility. She seemed to be able to read their minds. 'Who is this? Why did she have to come and waste our time today? Our responsibilities are meticulously planned. Not too many or a few chores so that our bosses can't lift a finger at us. They would even cover for each other, perhaps protecting a colleague so that nobody could be punished, using peer pressure to force them to accomplish certain jobs, and cunningly leaving some chores until the next shift arrives.

'The Bergie can wait until the next shift before we'll clean his wound.' To strip his clothes and uncover his layers of filth would take a lot of their precious time and keep them from their routine work. Only when the other patients in the ward complain about the stench will they capitulate and tackle the daunting task.

In Thandi's culture, it's disrespectful to look straight into their elder's eyes. While staring at her new black shoes, Sister Bothma's sarcastic voice reaches her through a tunnel. 'Well, well, let's see what our new health care worker is capable of. Nurse Witbooi, show Thandi what you do every day. Let her shadow you.'

She followed the nurse into an eight-bed male ward. Each patient laying there immediately recognised her as a rookie and kept a wary watch on her. With their collective eyes, she could feel her blue skirt being pulled from her waist. They then unbuttoned her white, long-sleeved shirt and without hesitation, unfastened her bra. Finally, her white panty was discarded on the heap of clothes. Next, they tied her hands behind her back, leaving her defenceless.

'You! Thandi! Come here.' Nurse Witbooi's flat voice breaks the spell, and she looks down at her blue skirt covering her calves. 'Help me take the patient's body temperature. I'll write it down on the charts if you read the figures.'

She passes her the glass stick that she took out from under a man's armpit.

'Come on. What's his temperature? We don't have all day.' Thandi's hands were shaking so violently that she feared she might drop the precious stick to the floor, where it would surely fall to pieces. She forces herself to read the figure on the stick and squints her eyes. But all she can read is the word "thermometer." *At least I can read. In fact, I did very well at school. Didn't my teacher tell me that my grades were adequate for admission to medical school?*

That evening, when she told her parents what the teacher had said, they laughed and reprimanded her. 'Daughter, daughter, you were born to be a mother. That is your highest duty. We need children to make us wealthy. In the meantime, you need to be the best helper you can. A doctor! Ha! Think about all those years of studying before you can bring home money to help your brother and sister with their studies. No, Thandi. Stop those idle thoughts. If you were a boy, it would've been different. But a woman's place is at home, where she can be a mother who will help her elderly parents one day.'

She squinted her eyes, willing them to read the figures that were supposed to be on the glass stick with the silver head. *This must be a joke. It's not funny, though.* 'There is nothing to read here, nurse.' She manages a weak smile, feeling relief that she's not exposed as an idiot.

'Here. Hand it to me. Just as I thought. Nobody has taught you anything. She can't even read a thermometer. Go stand by the window in the light and turn it around until you see a line.'

Thankfully, the men lost interest in her when their breakfast arrived. She stood there, turning, and twisting the glass stick that was called a "thermometer".

'Nurse Witbooi,' a voice boomed across the beds from the end of the row. Don't you think the spider webs should be cleared in this ward? It's disgusting how filthy this place is.'

'Excuse me, sir. Are you going to tell me how to run this ward?' Nurse Witbooi was taken aback and quickly forgot about Thandi, who was still battling to identify the illusive black line.

'If you knew who I am, you wouldn't ask that question.' Thandi looks up to see who was talking.

'I'm sorry, sir. To the best of my knowledge, you are the patient with hormone difficulties whose breasts started to develop and who is being operated on today. I'm not sure why spider webs are bothering you when you're due for a breast reduction.' Nurse Witbooi offers her hand to Thandi to take the thermometer from her and turns her back on the patient. Thandi ignores her. She must find the line first.

'Since I've been a patient in this ward, I've already prepared two letters of complaint regarding the nursing staff's misconduct. If you continue to be unpleasant, I'll put you on my list.' The patients were quiet; nobody dared to move. Thandi heard a bell ringing in another ward.

'I'm the secretary of the General Hospital Board of Directors and I must warn you that I take my job very seriously. I expect you to respect me and follow my instructions.'

Thandi ventured to glance away from the thermometer and back at the man with the deep voice. *Oh, he is the one wearing the red Mickey Mouse pyjamas. His breasts are huge. I wonder if he had to wear a bra.*

'You! What's your name again? Thandi! Fetch a duster in the utility room and clear the cobwebs.'

A solid black line develops on the glass stick as nurse Witbooi rushes out of the ward.

'Nurse! Nurse! His temperature is 40 degrees Celsius. He must be very sick. She yelled, but her words were cut off by Nurse Witbooi's rigid back.

*****

After lunch, nurse Witbooi instructs her to get two beds ready for new patients. She had to wash the covered mattresses and the metal frames of the beds. For this task, she was told to wear thick rubber gloves. *How does one work while wearing gloves? Mama would laugh if she saw this spectacle. I'm sure she has never worked wearing gloves.*

'Go to the scrub room and fetch hot water in a basin. It's the second door to the left. Hurry.'

Thandi enters the scrub room and turns on the hot water tap. *I wish I could go back to school, but perhaps staying at home would be preferable. Starting today, I'll be more helpful to Mama.* She wondered if she shouldn't just leave the hospital and never return. It's so hard to be told what to do all the time. And that thing with the thermometer! She has never been so humiliated in her life.

Somebody enters the scrub room. Thandi jumps as the door banged shut. Did it get locked? *Nurse Witbooi! Probably checking on me to see whether I can fill a bowl with hot water.* The presence in the room didn't feel good, but despite that, Thandi looked into the mirror above the basin to see herself smile at the ridiculous nurse. She jerked her head around and then froze. Standing behind her, so close that she could smell his unwashed body, stood one of the men she noticed in the men's ward. He was dressed in the hospital's blue night gown. It opened at the back, and she assumed he wore nothing underneath. Thandi was convinced he was the one who winked at her so familiarly that she cringed.

Within seconds, his hands were all over her body. Before she could shout out in shock, his hand covered her mouth. Adrenaline overtook her, and she disconnected from her body. The buttons of her white shirt flew across the tiled scrub room floor like scared birds flying from their nest. Her panties adorned her ankles like a broken bead necklace. She saw his naked feet from the position he held her, bent over, while expertly spreading her legs. She had to remember that his toenails were long and uncut. Water from the flowing tap sprayed over her neck as she was pressed harshly against the basin. *Nurse Witbooi will be upset because I left the tap running. My name is Thandi. I'm a helper.*

His powerful physique held her captive. It was as though an assegai had entered her body. Her shocked gasp of pain was muffled by the grunting noises the man made. His convulsions ended as abruptly as they began. He released his grip on her mouth and abruptly let go of her limp body. She heard somebody crying; the sound blended with the splashing water from the open tap.

Her white shirt was drifting on the dam of water, moving towards the opening beneath the door. A trickle of blood dripping onto her new black shoes brought her back to reality.

'What's happening here? Why is water running into the passage?'

Thandi knew her shame would be exposed once the door opened. 'What happened to you? Oh no! Were you attacked?' Nurse Witbooi's instincts takes over, and she grabs a clean sheet from the shelf to cover the trembling, semi-naked girl.

*****

It didn't take the nurse long to analyse the situation. During her twenty-year tenure at this hospital, she experienced many inconceivable things. Not much could shock her. But this happened directly under her nose, on her watch. It was unfathomable. The poor girl. Although she also didn't

approve of a novice shadowing her all day, she would never have wished something like this on her worst enemy.

'Who did this to you? Come on, girl. I must know!' She motions towards the door, not expecting a response from the trembling girl. 'Let's go to Trauma. They will take care of everything. I'll tell them to give you a tranquiliser. How fortunate that you're already in the hospital! If your mother had to bring you in now, you would've had to wait for a few hours before they would attend to you. A doctor should see you soon.'

'No. No. Please, let me go home. I'm not going to Trauma. I'll be fine. Please don't make a fuss.' Finally, the tears find their way into the proper channels. Thandi's heart was filled with a chilly, clammy feeling of hopelessness.

'I'm sorry, my girl, but this was a terrible crime committed here in our hospital. The horrible man who did this to you will have to pay for his evil deed. You could be infected with HIV for all we know! What happens if you get pregnant? No, no, Thandi. Don't argue with me.'

The word "pay" makes Thandi come to her senses. What happened to her wasn't just shocking and painful; it had consequences. Papa always warned her to stay pure and never let a man touch her until one day when she was married. The lobola! A virgin's parents get paid much more, and a pretty girl could fetch a substantial amount. Her whole life and future were ruined today; she could just as well have been killed with the knife she saw gleaming in the man's pocket. Then, she remembers her mother's sisis talking about men with aids who rape virgins believing they were a cure for their disease. Is this what happened to her today, exchanging her health and virginity for his HIV?

If only I could switch places with Mr. Umfadi, who is about to die. Is this the reason why he takes those grey pills? Is that good for relieving pain and removing the fear of death? Yes, I'll accompany nurse Witbooi to the doctor. Maybe he can give me something to ease the pain.

*****

It all took a very long time. They had to first open a file for her. Then she too had to play musical chairs on the bucket seats at trauma. One chair closer, one chair closer, sit, stand, sit, stand. Did the other patients know why she was there? Could they figure out why she was upset? Wrapped in a hospital sheet with blood on her shoes, her lip swollen from when it was held against the metal basin, tears streaking her face, she must have looked an awful sight.

The police officers openly took the brown box labelled "sexual assault" to the examining room. The seal was only opened when she was lying on the narrow bed behind the blue curtains.

She had died already. They could do with her whatever they pleased. Somehow, she wasn't concerned about dying anymore. Death seemed preferable to this humiliation. She only got scared when she realised that the pathway in her brain that was labelled "future" and "life" now only exposed a chasm that said "nowhere".

Maybe seventeen years of dreams were enough. Maybe she would be spared the "hoping for a better future" stuff. Always waiting, always waiting. Promises were made. The President said they would get work, nice houses, and better lifestyles. She has decided – she won't be a helper anymore. People must help themselves.

'Did you see the man who did this to you? Could you see his face? Why did he follow you to the scrub room? What did you wear? Did you in any manner encourage him?' The policeman sits with his pen in his hand, encouraging her to speak.

'No. No. No,' she replies feebly. 'Can I go home now, please?'

'You can go once you've had an injection to protect you against infections. Go, wait on a chair with the others, and the nurse will call you.'

Despite the shock and pain, she takes an interest in the other waiting patients. Elizabeth Taylor grinned from ear to ear when she hobbled off on her crutches. 'I can go home after six months in this place.' Thandi saw her getting into the waiting taxi at the exit.

Jafta Jantjies, who was dying of cancer, was supported by his church's elders. 'We'll pray till the bitter end, Brother Jantjies. We're here to keep your arms raised. God is good; he won't abandon you.'

The elderly lady in the wheelchair was assisted by her daughter, who stood behind her. The other daughter was standing outside near the window, attracting lots of attention. 'Why are you still standing there by our mother? Shouldn't she be lying in a bed by now? It's 8 o'clock already and what have the doctors done for her? These doctors should be able to work considerably faster if they studied to be real doctors.'

Thandi could feel the dread brought on by collective pain come on her like a frightening storm. They acted like wounded animals after being forced to sit together for many anxious hours. The morphine dose given to the man in the grey hat begins to act after ten minutes, and his wailing stopped. *If only I could go to sleep like that. What happened to me today will stay with me forever. I'll never return to this place.*

When the cops accompany a cuffed man to the waiting police van outside, the other patients surrounding her gasp. Thandi was just in time to observe the tattoos on his back and thighs, revealed by the opening flaps of his blue hospital gown. *That's him. At least the police believed me.*

*****

They sent her home by ambulance. The hospital administrator had a lot to say about legal action, claims, and all kind of damages to be paid. She blocked her ears and refused to listen or comment. The police have her address. They will notify her if she's required to testify in court.

If only I could wash myself now. The policewoman said I could take a bath; they have taken all the samples they needed for the investigation to bring a case against the man. How will I explain to Mama why the buttons are torn off my shirt? I'm so ashamed.

As the ambulance approached the entrance to the township, she noticed a dark figure with a stick and a rucksack. Mr. Umfadi! Did it take all this time to get his pills?

When he heard her approaching footsteps, he stops to lean on his stick. 'Is that you, Thandi? You worked late today? How was your first day? I hoped I could see you at the General.' Mr. Umfadi turned to face her. He was convinced something was wrong with his neighbour's daughter. This morning, she looked bright-eyed and bushy-tailed, her eyes filled with dreams and desires. Why is her face streaked with tears now, her braids untidy, and her shirt unbuttoned?

'What happened to you, Thandi?' he enquired. He watched in dismay as her eyes filled with tears. This was the first time today that somebody took an interest in her and showed sympathy. She could feel her composure crumble and contemplated telling him about the terrible thing that stole her dreams today in a place where she would have become a helper.

'Mr. Umfadi. Something terrible happened at the General today. But don't tell my mama. They've already taken the horrible man to the police station. Please don't worry; I'll be all right.'

'Oh no, Thandi. That's terrible. Why did it have to happen to you of all people?'

Mr. Umfadi? What's the matter? Why are you so pale?'

'Please my child. Help me. Can you call an ambulance? I'm not feeling well. I think I'm going to die tonight.'

It all happened as if in slow motion, and afterwards she remembered how the colour of his eyes changed into a strange glimmer, the sound his body made when it hit the ground; how the dust moved upward from the ground; and then settled again on his outstretched broken body. Finally, his stick fell onto his chest.

'Mr. Umfadi! Please don't die now. I love you. Wait here. I'm going to ask Mama to call the ambulance. Maybe they can turn around to fetch you. They can't be too far away yet.

*****

Mama was too busy calling the ambulance and tending to Mr. Umfadi to notice that she looked different. She quickly slipped into the washroom, took off her clothes, and slid into the warm bath water, which her siblings just abandoned.

'Thandi! Help me, please. Agnes won't give me my towel. Tell her to give it to me!

She smiled at her sister, took a deep breath, and slid deeper into the tub to immerse her head and whole body. *How long will it take before I drown?* And then she wondered if her mother could buy her a thermometer. If she could practice finding the black line on the glass stick, she could show Nurse Witbooi that she's not stupid. Her tight muscles relaxed gradually, and she felt a strange sensation descend upon her. Hope – pure, undulated hope – made her realise that tomorrow could only be better than today.

As soon as Mr. Umfadi returns from the hospital, she'll help him get strong again.

*****

Agent Beware

He had to admit that he hadn't been prepared for the beauty of the coastal route. When he boarded the bus in Cape Town, he made sure the destination said, "Port Elizabeth." Not knowing where he wanted to disembark, made the trip unpredictable but exciting. When he bought the ticket, he made sure that he would sit next to the window. This trip was completely different from that long drive from Pretoria through the desolate Karoo. He never once considered doing his business in any of the towns they drove through. It's quite sad to see how much effect the depopulation of the "platteland" had. The streets looked desolate, and some homes were boarded up. *Where had the people gone? Were they homing pigeons like him?* he pondered.

It's hard to resist the temptation to get sentimental, something he seldom allows himself to succumb to. Below the rocks of the small mountain pass, he can see the white crests of waves crashing onto the golden beach. Where are the people? Why is nobody swimming?

What is that lovely smell drifting through the open bus window? He has never smelt something so haunting. He vaguely remembers his grandmother telling him about her father, who fought in the Boer War as a horseman, that the fodder for the horses had to be sent by ship from England. Yes. That smell is from the plants that were "sown" here as dropping horse feed.

It's not only plants that he is smelling. There is something more familiar, reaching his nostrils. He smells money too. He slips lower into the uncomfortable seat to enhance his view of the massive homes he spotted perched on the cliffs. The youngster sitting next to him moves slightly in his sleep. What a shame young folks don't appreciate nature. He probably danced all night at a club, and now he is too tired to realise he's driving through Paradise.

This trip is going to be different. He could decide where he wanted to stay. It's not as if he was on a vacation. No, this was strictly business. Admittedly, he would have liked to stay longer in Cape Town. It was a pity he got involved in an argument with that young man at the Backpackers. It's not as if he was forced to flee, but he didn't realise that the close-knit community of dropouts covered each other's backs. He always tries to avoid the police. Been there, done that. Leaving Pretoria was hard enough, and he is determined to turn over a new leaf.

'Our next stop will be in twenty minutes.' The bus driver is efficient, and they seem to be on time. He puts the information pack he found at the bus station in his backpack. In it, he read about this town. He must soon make a few decisions. *Will I get off at the next town?* His legs are stiff, and his back is aching. These seats aren't designed to accommodate tall people. *Yes, let's call it a day. If I don't like this place, I'll find a lift to Knysna tomorrow. It all depends on how many estate agencies there are in this small town.*

As the bus slows down, he realises he must make up his mind about his identity. *What will he call himself? Should it be an Afrikaans or English name? What about something foreign for a change, like Hans Schwabe, for instance? I have often been mistaken for being German, thanks to my Afrikaans accent.*

'Please make sure you take all your luggage,' says the moustached bus driver as he manoeuvres the bus into the designated parking area for buses. *Sure Mate. Don't worry. I travel light as it is.*

The youngster's bag with his new trainers will come in handy too. The shoes probably won't fit him, but they might be used as a bargaining tool in future. As he gets up from the seat, he glances at the boy's sleeping face. He looks so innocent with his stockinged foot tucked underneath his bottom. It's hard to hide the smirk on his face when he thinks of the boys' surprise when he wakes up in Port Elizabeth without his bag in sight.

*****

He noticed the crude "Backpackers" signage on a white wall as the bus waited at the traffic light to change to green. That will be his first stop since he left Cape Town earlier this morning.

Okay. I've decided. I'll be Roger Green, and I am from the UK. South Africa is part of my world tour, which should last ten months. His next destination would be the Great Wall of China, then Russia, Antarctica, South America, and wherever else I fancy to go. This is such an amazing town that I would like to make it my future home. What is that protruding rock in the west called again? Oh, I'm sure it is Lubbe's point, or is it Graham? As soon as I have settled down, I must read the brochure again. Bottom line is that walking is my passion, and I've heard there are tracks in the forests that are very popular with amblers.

'How did you get here, sir? Asks the receptionist at the backpackers. 'You may park your car at the back of the building. It will be safe there.' The girl has long brown hair that reaches her middle. She wears a bikini top, and a sarong

85

covers her legs. This is indeed a holiday town. 'You are welcome to join us for a barbeque tonight. The other visitors are all getting together to make a bonfire at seven o'clock. Bring your drinks and meat, and we'll take care of the rest.'

"Roger" can't believe his ears. This is the perfect opportunity to meet people and hear the town's gossip. He doesn't always have enough time to make his hit, so he needs all the help he can get. Quick in and quick out with his prize in his pocket.

He expects to be questioned about why he travels by bus, a slow and inconvenient, but cheaper option than by car. 'I make use of public transport as often as possible. That's the best way to meet people and to get to know the locals' customs. In London, I have a chauffeur who drives me around. To be honest, many people who grow up in cities in Europe never learn to drive. Public transportation is excellent, and parking is a huge problem. I spend a lot of time in the Caribbean, and to get there, my private jet is always on standby.

*****

The girl at reception shows him the bonfire outside in the private, enclosed area. There are already six other people sitting on seats placed in a circle. They each hold a drink in their hands. Their friendliness surprises him. He could easily fit in here. Hopefully they have enough food for him too.

'Are they Rastafarians?' Roger asks, impolitely pointing at three men sitting opposite him.

'What makes you ask that?' enquires the short guy seated next to him.

'Their hair. I've never seen so many people with dreadlocks in one place.'

'It's convenient if you are a fisherman.'

'Oh. That makes sense.'

Maybe these people aren't quite the right group for my goal. Nevertheless, I'll question them. If they're drunk enough, their lips wouldn't be sealed.

'Which estate agency is the most successful in this town? I'm here to buy property, and I want to do business with the best agents.' They must realise he isn't an ordinary guy. Experience is what counts, and he has done this so many times before. Tonight is Sunday. Tomorrow, the party begins. *Act casually and play on human tendencies and weaknesses. Greed, money, and success go hand in hand.*

*****

The backpackers' building isn't far from the main road, where many estate agencies' offices adorn the sidewalks. Walking there won't attract attention. Unless somebody asks where his car is, nobody would guess he arrived here with a bus.

His first point of contact is with one of the more well-known companies. Yes, they do have stunning properties for sale with sea views. They also have a beautiful resort on their books which has just come on the market.

'Would you like to view it right now?' asks the girl with the spectacles. It's a pity she isn't attractive. He regards the physical attraction he develops with a pretty lady add to the excitement he feels during the 'chase' for the perfect property. 'Give me a few minutes to call and arrange for a viewing.'

'Yes, sure. I can go right away.' So far, so good. Not too many questions were asked. She seems to take him at face value.

While drinking the strong coffee and enjoying the flavours of the freshly baked milk tart she presented; he has an opportunity to study the girl. He can tell from the tone of her voice, that she's excited. If she had to take off her spectacles and put on lipstick, she will be pretty. Perhaps he should invite her out for supper. She'll have to pay though because he will forget his wallet at his hotel. Too bad.

I have seen all this before. The look in her eyes, the trembling fingers, the slight aggression when she speaks to the receptionist 'Try again. They must be home!'

Oh, how lovely to watch. This is not quite what I had in mind, but only a warming-up experience. Nevertheless, my heart is pounding like an actor about to recite Shakespeare in front of a packed hall.

'Please excuse my dirty car. I didn't have time to wash it after it stood outside all weekend.' He is sitting next to the woman whose perfume he finds overwhelming in the confines of her car. He enjoys seeing her discomfort as she wriggles in the seat. She seems very anxious but relaxes once they arrive at the resort.

'The resort is 25 hectares and has mooring for small leisure boats. There are 10 chalets for rent and in the main building there is a restaurant. Let me show you the interior of one of the chalets.'

So far, so good. It's important that he show some interest at this point.

'These paintings. Are they included in the sale?' He enquires. 'They are all reproductions, of course, but I would love it to be included in the deal.' He knows he could impress her with his knowledge of art.

'No worries. I'll ask the seller. If you are interested, the adjacent resort is also on the market. Unfortunately, another agency has a sole mandate, but we often work together, and I can ask them to show you the property.'

He makes up his mind. Of course, he'll buy them both. His staff must stay on a smallholding in the area, as it's never a good idea to have them live on the premises where he stays. Maybe he should also buy the extravagant house on the beachfront. And what about the other mansion next to it? Is that on the market, and if not, will she please inquire about the possibility of buying it?

The spectacled girl trembles in anticipation of all the possibilities. This is the moment Roger loves. The world is his oyster, and he knows how to play his audience.

Tomorrow, they'll certainly go on a trip on the Featherbed pleasure boat. *I'll have a starter of fresh sea oysters followed by Steak au Poivre, and then I'll round it off with crème brulé. Mm mm. Is there an easier profession to touch?*

*****

The second office is a bit classier. It's modern and furnished with white desks, and many original paintings decorate the walls. They are a well-known franchise, and he realises he'll have to be on high alert. The salespeople have all gone to list an open house, but the receptionist calls someone, and after she tells the other person there is a prospective client to buy a few upmarket properties he can hear a shift in their conversation. She puts some pressure on the person on the other side of the line. 'I think you should come straight away, Brian. Yes, he sounds serious.'

Within minutes, a white BMW parks in front of the office. A neatly dressed middle-aged man walks inside, followed by a lady wearing a polka-dot skirt and a white shirt. Without being told, he realises they are a couple.

This hit might be a bit more challenging. He notices how the estate agent checks out his clothes, his watch, his shoes. Be careful now: he must watch what he says. This man has experience with human behaviour and personality types. Today, like meets like. His heart starts to pound, and he can feel little rivulets of perspiration run down his back. He looks forward to this challenge, like a bull gauging the matador with the red flag.

Brian is also an experienced traveller. He lived in London for a few years and knows the streets he mentioned. The questions he asks are too specific. Sensing danger, his heart beats even faster.

'Do you want a cup of coffee? Or water? You seem quite hot. Brenda, can you please bring Roger a cup of coffee. Roger, may I please make a copy of your ID or passport? We always do this with our clients to approve them as bone fide buyers. Our sellers get very annoyed if we use their properties as a soundboard to offset other properties.'

'I'm sorry, Brian, but I left my passport at the Backpackers. Will it be okay if I show it to you later this afternoon?' *This could be problematic, though.*

His usual line about the economy and the reason why he thought the country was going to flourish despite politics doesn't go down very well. Surprisingly, the couple knows a lot about the deciduous fruit industry in the Western Cape, and he starts to see red lights warning him to play it cool. Maybe the five apple farms he bought in Elgin last week were a tad too many.

He must give the man his due. He was a true gentleman. Although he did take him to the other resort where the company had a sole mandate, when they returned to the office, he could sense that his charade was going to end there. Brian wasn't interested in the property consortium he was going to start. Even the possibility of becoming his portfolio manager and future related business trips to Europe didn't appeal to him. Although he confirmed that his passport was in order, the usual flicker of the eye was absent. It would be best to call it a day and move on further down the street to another, maybe smaller, agency.

*****

Tonight, he wants to stand in the street outside one of the houses he was shown today. Maybe the homeowner recognises him as the prospective buyer of their house. He didn't intend to make them too nervous, but he would love to smell the scent of their panic. *I must remember to tell the estate agent tomorrow that I'll be delighted if they throw in their furniture too.*

'What is he doing here at this time of night? Do you think he wants to buy our house?' The homeowner will ask.

'What do you say, darling? Should we put in an offer on that apartment we viewed in Jefferey's Bay? Oh, gosh. We don't want to be caught with our pants down our ankles. The agent said he was a multibillionaire; why would he even want to buy our house?'

His guess was that after a few more days in this town, he'd have to move again. The owner of the backpackers has lately been more insistent about the outstanding payment for the room. He might be able to stall him for another day or two, but then he'll have to do his usual disappearing act. Whereto, he wasn't sure yet.

Ultimately, he would like to move into a suitable property for which he would sign an offer to purchase, subject to the successful transfer of money from abroad. The occupational interest will be minimal, as his generous "deposit" should provide ample proof of his intentions.

He was still toying with the idea whether he should return to one of the other coastal towns he noticed on their drive here or whether he should move closer to Port Elizabeth. Whatever direction he chooses, there are thousands more estate agents who will bow to his charming ways. *Maybe I should change my name to something more elegant.*

*****

Shangri-La

It is one thing to live in a scenic mountain community, but there is a disadvantage to this fenced-in, yet beautiful, valley. The valley basin would get unbearably hot in the summer. However, piercing cold gusts would flow down from the crests at times, forcing one to dress up snugly in thick artic coats and scarves in winter. The dampness that penetrates to the marrow of one's bones isn't mentioned in tourist guidebooks. In the winter, driving rain and icy cold winds are a part of life in this stunning region.

There are also minor annoyances, such as when you absolutely need something from a store only to be told that it's unavailable since most people drive to the neighbouring town to buy it there. Certain bureaucratic conveniences and services are unavailable, making life difficult for farm labourers who must catch a bus on a Saturday to get proviant. Despite this, there are a few off-sales and bars – far too numerous for such a small town.

Something happened to her there. Despite the joy she derived from her children, it was as if the mountains conspired to choke her. How is it possible that nature and beauty could extract vision and hope for the future out of someone so young and full of dreams? She had a good life, but is this it now? Is this the life she wants?

It was a small world, far too small for her liking. Here she was known not as Alice but as the mother of Rita, Sonia, and Bennie, as well as the wife of Donald, the prosperous farmer of La Gratitude. The Stepford Wives impact was still evident in the women of the 1970s and even more so in the farming community, where the farmers would regularly meet to discuss the pending crop and the conditions for the upcoming grape harvest while the wives had to entertain themselves.

She was aware, even as a young wife, that her responsibility would be to support her husband. But not as a team, more like two horses harnessed with opposing visions. 'My mother was always working, and I hated returning home from school to an empty house,' Donald said. 'I'd rather have you here at home to be close to the children and keep an eye on the household.'

Ironically, as a couple, they played a great game of league tennis. Despite their inability to connect as husband and wife, they beat opponents who should've wiped them out on the court. Their approach was unemotional, methodical, and brutal. They excelled with their relentless driving and lightning replies to their opponents' volleys and bluffs.

To her surprise, she was elected to the library committee, and she was charged with selecting books from the bus that comes every three months. Reading good books brought her a lot of joy, and she frequently had to force herself to put one away when she had to do a chore.

When Donald was elected chair of the local National Party, she became the secretary, making Donald's job easier. Though she had many responsibilities, her life seemed to revolve around the farm and the community, particularly the farm labourers and their families who required a lot of uplifting.

Who was she, despite all the local plaudits and titles? Where was she heading? Maybe the answer could be found beyond the peaks. If only she could develop her own identity, separate from the stream of lava dragging her in a certain way and pressuring her to conform. She had a road to travel from this valley, but it was still to come.

*****

Today she had to do some chores in the neighbouring town. Even though it's only a thirty-kilometre journey from their property, she enjoys the independence of a solo trip. She's struck by the beauty of her surroundings. It's impossible to be dismissive of the magnificent mountain ranges, vineyards, fruit trees, and woodlands. She's awestruck by the white, historic Cape Dutch homes that have been meticulously kept and restored by the descendants of French Huguenot's and Dutch settlers.

Her car purrs smoothly along the tarred road. She feels good today. 'I am a Bolander in every part of my being,' she verifies to herself. This is where I was meant to be born, and we are fortunate to raise our children where their forefathers lived.'

The thought of her children makes her feel especially good. The girls were so bright, eagerly drinking in all the opportunities life was offering. Bennie was only a toddler, and it pained her to leave him in the care of his nanny. If he had enjoyed the drive in the car with her, she would gladly have brought him with her, but he prefers to stay with Donald, whom he could follow around on the farm. He has many friends there. They are the children of the farm labourers who play in the orchards while their mothers pick fruit or prune the trees. Should it be a rainy day, he would happily build Lego towns in his bedroom while listening to music.

She would never let him roam around alone on the farm; however, they kept an eye on him because he had a habit of fleeing from the house. Farms are infamous for mishaps, especially among young children who lack a sense of risk. Tractors often race around the corner of a building and might appear without warning in clouds of dust. A bubbling mountain stream near their home turns into a raging mini river in the winter. These thoughts make her shudder, but she quickly shrugs them off to settle into the ride along the main street of their neighbouring town.

But her thoughts return to the unsettling dream she had last night. How strange was it that she felt compelled to tell her best friend not to allow her little son to play outside their back door today? What could it be that worries her so much? Maybe when they meet again, she'll suggest that they build a sandpit for the child close to their back door. Cathy might think she's neurotic, but at least she'll feel she has done her duty. Lately, she has been having such strange dreams. She wasn't sure what to make of this event, having been raised in a rigorous Calvinistic household, and she shrugs aside the recollection of the dream once more. It was as if Divinity was foretelling her future. *Oh damn! Stop your nonsense, she scolds herself. Maybe I'll phone Cathy tonight to tell her about my sandpit idea.*

*****

Why did she hesitate? Things may have turned out very differently if she had followed through on her dream. The toddler would have grown up to become a tall young man, delighting his adoring parents. Cathy recently married Johan, a well-known farmer in the area. To the residents who frown upon divorce and remarriage, she's a bit of a mystery. Members of the conservative Afrikaans-speaking community, who were mainly Dutch Reformed Churchgoers, battled to understand this strong-willed, outspoken English-speaking woman from Cape Town.

There was quite a stir a few weeks ago when the church council had to decide whether the English-oriented bank should handle the church account, even though they provided better service and a higher interest rate. Afrikaners must band together, or what? What worked for their parents should work for them, right?

Their rationale made no sense to Alice. She was patriotic and loved her language and culture, but she wasn't willing to die on the stakes for it. Other cultures and points of view piqued her interest, and she desired to learn more. That could explain why she found Cathy to be such a breath of fresh air. Though she was taught that divorce was a major sin, she learned in her Bible study group that judging someone was also not acceptable.

Her husband has never confronted her because she visits other denominations. He could easily have forbidden her to join their prayer groups, since he certainly must have had reservations. What should he tell his friends and council members about his wife's fraternising with the new religious views brought by the incomers? To them, tradition is everything; didn't they descend from the French Huguenots, who sacrificed everything to bring their faith, religion, vine shoots, and agricultural knowledge to this country and valley?

Lately she has become very stressed. She is caught between a rock and a hard place. Her dissatisfaction with her single-minded and traditional friends deepens by the day. Since she's made friends with people who share her passion for a loving God who reveals other dimensions of himself, her mother has expressed concern that she's spending less time with her and more with the members of her charismatic groups. Is this then the price one must pay to grow closer to God? She's perplexed. Perhaps this is evidence that she's on the right track. *Doesn't the Bible say one should bear one's cross and sacrifice friends and family?*

She parks their station waggon in the shade of a large oak tree. There wasn't too much time to wander around town today; she had to pick up her daughters from school in a few hours.

As she walks towards the shop, her strides are long and determined. *It's a shame I must drive so far to find a zipper in the proper shade!* The shoe shop is around the corner, and she's looking forward to meeting the girl who works there. She always shops there for shoes and the assistant knows exactly what she likes.

Oh no! Why do I keep running into people from our town? I really don't have time to talk to Janet and Robbie today, despite how much I care about them. The pair is active in their "renewal group" and has been very supportive of her search for a new spiritual path. It's clear that they are glad to see her, though they look serious and troubled. She stops in front of the couple under the canopy hanging above the shop window.

'You won't believe what happened, Alice. It's so terrible; we're in shock. We don't have much time as we're on our way to Tygerberg Hospital.'

'What happened? Please tell me.' Her heart starts beating faster, and the colour drains from her face. *Please, God, let my family be safe.* She doesn't know what she'd do if something had to happen to one of her loved ones. Instinctively, she reaches out to grab Janet's arm. This news was going to be something bad – something out of the ordinary.

'Cathy had to rush Tommy to the hospital. A vehicle ran over him on their farm. He suffered severe head injuries and is on life support. Doctors are fighting for his life.' Janet's face contorts as she blurts out this information, as if she were spewing poisonous food.

Alice sees the colour red. Despite the summer heat, her legs are shaky, and ice-cold fingers wriggle across her face. This is unreal. Why do Janet and Robbie believe this sensational story? In any event, how did they find out about this? There's no time to obtain additional information because the couple has already left.

I need to get to Cathy in the hospital. She'll need my support. After unlocking the car, she throws her parcels on the passenger seat. Maybe she should go home first to see if her family is okay. Yes, she must remember to collect the girls from the school. Perhaps Donald has heard about the incident already, and he would be able to fill her in. News travels fast in their small community.

Her mind races as she drives home. A few hours ago, she marvelled at the beauty of the scenery. Now she doesn't notice anything. Yesterday, she looked after the beautiful twenty-month-old boy with the blue eyes and blond curly hair while his parents went to a funeral. How's it possible that he is now lying in a hospital cot connected to tubes, his head distorted, and his eyes swollen? No, she still needs confirmation before she believes the news. How on earth could this have happened?

Yesterday as they were playing in the pool, she was thinking about Tommy's future. What would his life be like? His father was already fifty-two years old, and his siblings were all in their twenties. Surely, he would live a prosperous life as their special child, their dream-come- true son who would keep them young and their love for each other alive. And now this has happened!

Her own son was a typical boy who adored his father. How lucky was he to go everywhere with his dad – on the tractor or the motorbike, in the truck driving around on the farm? If he had to choose, he would always prefer to be with his father. Maybe one day, when he was older, they would have a special friendship, and he would share his dreams and ideals with her.

Alice is reminded of her father's death a few years ago, and she's unsure how she'll deal with tragedy when faced with it again. Her parent's early death was a shock, but it was also a godsend. She was saddened when her grandparents died, but she understood it was unavoidable and part of life's cycle. Their neighbour's little girl, drowned in their dam a few years ago, which was heartbreaking. But nothing like this. This is so close. It's her friend's baby, and she looked after him yesterday. Was the dream she had a premonition, a warning of things to come?

The girls are already waiting at the gate of the school when she arrives. She notices small groups of parents standing close together. They are probably discussing the accident. The news of the tragedy must be spreading through the community like wildfire.

Donald agrees that she should go to the hospital to support Cathy and her husband. She kisses her children. She takes mental snaps of their faces as if to safeguard them. Holding them against her, she feels tears welling up in her eyes. 'Donald, please look after them. I'm not sure when I'll be home again. It's possible that I'll be late. Do your homework, girls, and make sure your brother takes a bath.'

'Don't worry, miss Alice. I'll prepare supper for them.' Alma, their nanny, has been with them since they were born. In many ways, she's a better mother to them than she is.

'Thanks, Alma. I know that between you and their dad, they'll be safe.

In her heart of hearts, she only wants to run away from it all.

*****

The waiting room at the hospital is large. There are comfortable chairs arranged in circles. In the corner, there is a television. This is different from other waiting rooms. The parents and family of paediatric emergencies need special comforts. She didn't expect to see so many people from their prayer group. *How did they manage to get here before me? Where is Cathy? I must see her right away.* The odour of antiseptic and sanitation products is overpowering. She sneezes. There is a vending machine in the corridor. She realises how thirsty she was. Since she left their home this morning, she's had nothing to eat or drink.

'Hello Alice. It's so nice of you to have come.' Cathy's familiar voice sounds like curdled cream. Alice turns around sharply. She embraces Cathy, and they hold each other tightly. The convulsions coming from Cathy match her own.

'What happened, Cathy? How come Tommy is currently fighting for his life in intensive care?' Alice feels sick to her stomach – if only she had called last night to share her premonition! Maybe this could have been avoided. She'd rather not mention it now. 'Shall we sit down, then you can tell me about it?'

'Later, darling. I'll tell you about it shortly. I want to join the prayer group now. Everyone gathered here is fasting

101

for the rest of the day. We don't want to be sad now. God is going to perform a miracle, don't you understand? He allowed this to happen so that he could show us how powerful he is.'

Alice feels like she's been thumped into her stomach. She's obviously out of touch with reality. Her practical mind wishes to allude to the spiritual aspect of the situation. How will she muster enough faith that a miracle is going to occur and that the injured baby will shortly awaken unhurt with all his mental faculties restored?

'Do you think I'll be permitted to visit Tommy?' She feels compelled to see the baby, to rub his podgy arm, or to stroke a golden curl on his head.

'Of course. Go through that door, and the nurse will take you to his bedside.'

*****

'Do you know how this happened, Thomas? I looked after this baby yesterday and would never have thought the next time I see him; he would be like this! How awful.' The sight of the baby lying on his back, with pipes and machines attached to his little broken body, is a sight Alice never expected to observe. Bandages cover his head, his eyes are swollen, and blue bruises decorate his torso like tattoos, showing where he was trampled by the tyres of a tractor, a truck, or maybe a car.

Thomas, the neighbour who found the body lying in the courtyard, approaches Alice to give her a hug. 'Apparently Cathy was getting ready to go to the shop when she realised Tommy wasn't inside the house anymore. They were all outside calling him when I arrived to borrow a plough. I joined the search and found him lying face down in front of the garage. Wheel tracks were clearly visible but has not been identified yet. Tthe baby was unresponsive. The doctor arrived quickly but realised he couldn't wait for an ambulance to arrive. He and Cathy who held Tommy on her lap raced to Tygerberg Hospital.'.

'Oh, my gosh! What a trip that must have been. What did the doctors say? Will he recover from this trauma?'

'They won't tell us too much – only that if his vitals don't stabilise by tomorrow morning, there isn't much to do for his survival. It seems a miracle is all we can pray for, Alice. Other than that, I'd suggest you give Cathy as much love and support as possible. I don't think the couple will leave the hospital until things change, either for the worse or the better.

'Then I'll stay here until tomorrow too.' Alice has made up her mind. She'll call Donald to tell him that she's needed here. It's obvious that prayer is the only way to get through the day and night. Maybe God will hear hers too.

*****

When she turns onto the National Road, rays of the sun coming up in the east blind her. Memories of the morning they drove home on this same road after her father died in the

Groote Schuur hospital flood her. She can still hear her mother's sobs, calling for her "Pally" who left her alone with four children.

This time she's driving back to her Shangri-La, knowing that once again they have lost something precious. Their prayers haven't been answered. Luckily, science and the doctors knew when trying to prolong life would become a mockery. This baby was brain dead, probably since after the accident. Their prayers throughout the day and night were to make his parents brave enough to accept the inevitable. They had to release him; let him go to his own paradise.

103

It is quiet in the car. Alice has slowed down. She isn't in a hurry to get home. The moment she witnessed when the couple agreed with the doctor to put off the machine is replaying in her mind like a sickening tune. *What if they waited another twelve hours? Shouldn't they have trusted God more?* She is grateful that it wasn't her call to make.

Her family will wake up in an hour. The rays of the sun should bathe the vineyards in bright orange light as she drives down the lane towards their home, her Shangri-La.

*****

Feast of Tabernacles

It's past time for the oblivious woman to wake up. She discovers the existence of another universe with surprise. When one boards a plane, one could be transported to a magical place like a genie on a magic carpet. She had never considered travelling to other countries. Could she, however? Will she?

Her world has been surrounded by fictitious borders that hems her in. This is the Western Cape. She was born there, and she'll die there one day. She was fated to dwell in the village of her forefathers, as if her life had been orchestrated by a maestro. And it appears that this is the world her children will grow up in too.

'There is only one Biblical feast that Christians and Jews celebrate in Israel.'

Alice's interest is piqued immediately. Her inquiring mind grasps the knowledge presented by the preacher to the assembly. She pushes the hefty sleeping toddler on her lap into a more comfortable posture as she sits up. This is significant; she should take notes. What happened to her notebook?

'The Israelites were instructed to celebrate the end of their harvest season. At its core, the Feast of Tabernacles, or Sukkot, is a heavenly-instituted celebration designed to help the Children of Israel look towards the future and their coming salvation. Just as the Israelites sheltered in tabernacles in the wilderness, Jesus would one day dwell in a tabernacle of flesh. This feast is usually commemorated at the end of October, which is Autumn in Israel. Men would cut palm leaves to build huts where they would sleep. The Feast of Tabernacles celebration typically commences with an outdoor worship event where newly arrived pilgrims share a meal together under a full moon. It was Israel's Thanksgiving and a reminder of when God delivered Israel, through Moses, out of slavery in Egypt and their time in the wilderness or desert. The Israelites lived in tabernacles or booths on their 40-year journey to the Promised Land.'

It's hard to keep up with the teaching. She furiously scribbles down notes. Zechariah 14:16. That is the scripture she should read tonight. There it explains that "everyone who is left of all the nations which came against Jerusalem shall go up from year to year to worship the King, the Lord of hosts, and to keep the Feast of Tabernacles."

Now that she has this crucial text written down, she relaxes and sits back. The toddler yawns and wriggles his fat little body to find a more comfortable crevice in her thin body. Today, her two daughters joined their father to visit the Dutch Reformed Church, where they'll attend Sunday school. It's too bad he wasn't here today. She'll have to explain everything to him with her usual zeal. Will it, however, captivate him, the way she's stirred?

'They expect a huge return of Jews from the diaspora to Israel within the next few years in preparation for the coming of the Messiah.' This is up Alice's alley. 'Thousands of Jews will enter Finland to avoid Russian persecution.'

'This year, October 1981, we're organising a tour group to visit Israel during the Feast of Tabernacles. I'll place information pamphlets on the front table. Go home to pray about this. Do you have any questions?'

The lady sitting in front of Alice raises her hand. 'How much will it cost?'

'The flights, hotels, transport, and visa will amount to R5 000. Get your passports in order. If God wants you there, he'll make a way for you.' The preacher closes his Bible lying on the lectern and turns around to lead the congregation into singing the closing song. Though Alice is very interested, she's not sure if it would be quite as simple as that to raise funds.

*****

'I'm going on this tour, Alice. Nothing will stop me. Will you please accompany me?' Cathy dwarfs the girl standing next to her. She cuts a striking figure with her tall, thin body. Her shoulder-length blond hair frames her face and draws attention to her big blue eyes.

'I don't know, Cathy. What about my children? I can't leave them just like that. Donald needs me on the farm.'

'Oh, come on! Surely, he can let you go for ten days. What the heck! You know, Al, before you obey your husband, you must obey God.'

Alice feels her heart thumping. This could become a conundrum – wanting to please her husband while obeying God at the same time. The toddler clings to her and kicks her in the side. He is heavy, and she needs to get home. 'Where will I get the funds for the plane ticket, Cathy? It's not like we had a bumper crop and made a lot of money. We're not going to make it until the season begins.'

'We'll make a plan. Maybe my husband could lend you the money. Let's see. I need this after Timmy's accident, Alice. I must change my situation. It kills me to get up each morning, knowing he's gone for good.'

107

I'm hoping she doesn't get emotional right now. Cathy is still grieving the death of her baby, who died under weird and unexplained circumstances a few months ago. Somebody knows what happened that day when a vehicle crushed Timmy's head and tiny body, but that person isn't coming forward to admit guilt. With no witnesses, the detectives threw their hands up in despair.

It's evident she's made up her mind, and nothing will stop her from travelling to Israel in a few weeks. Around them small groups of people are chatting. It's as if a wildfire is spreading through the churchgoers standing around while holding mugs of coffee in their hands.

'I'm going to make an appointment to see the bank manager tomorrow.' She hears Bennie say. Obviously, Sally will accompany him on the tour; the couple does everything together, unlike her who longs to share her newfound faith with Donald. Oh well, one day he'll catch up with her and then they'll be a super team of believers.

'Bye, Cathy. I'll phone you later to tell you what Donald said about his wife's new outlandish idea. Ha ha!'

*****

She hasn't flown on a plane for ages, and she must admit that she's terrified of hights. What would happen if the plane should crash? She isn't ready to die yet; it's far too soon. It was difficult for her to leave her family behind but she's on a mission to visit the Holy Land. Gosh, she worked hard to get here. No, it would be disastrous if the plane had to crash. It helps to relieve her anxiety to chat to the strangers next to her. They are seasoned travellers and Alice decides to watch them and follow their example.

When the plane is about to take off, her thoughts turn to her suitcase, which is packed with fresh summer outfits for the hot Israeli climate. She spent hours preparing her outfits; buying patterns and fabric and sitting by the sewing machine convinced her that she was really going on this adventure. Her children have been left in capable hands. It helps that Donald is a farmer and will be available to fetch the girls from school and take them to their afternoon activities. Their fridge is covered in instructions and a daily itinerary of the period she'll be gone.

Something happens to her on that plane. To her surprise and shock, she becomes an individual. Cathy and the other members of their group is seated in a different section of the plane. She's seated amongst strangers. The reason that she's always positioned at the back of a queue might be because her surname starts with a "Z." Who knows if this is a foreshadowing of things to come?

Tonight, when she makes a remark, Donald isn't there to seek for confirmation. He isn't there to help her out when she can find the right word or loses track of her thoughts. Chatting to the friendly passengers sitting next to her in the Boeing heading for Frankfort, she finds she must complete her own sentences. *Are these people interested in me?* She looks around, astounded. *I am now the main primary character. Tonight, I'm not someone's wife or a mother, I'm just an individual woman on a quest to fulfil a void in my heart. It's okay. I may do this without guilt.*

Who would have predicted how difficult it would be to raise R5000? When her family and friends heard about her challenge, they put cash in her hand which she clutched tightly until she could deposit it into her newly opened savings account. She smiles as she recalls taking on the challenge of swimming two lengths of the public swimming pool in August while blankets of white snow covered the mountain peaks. 'I'll give you R200 if you complete two lengths of the pool.' She wasn't sure if Donald was pulling her leg.

'Oh, come on Donald, you know I hate cold water!'

'You'll have to be brave if you want to achieve your goal.' She should've known that even though he agreed to let her go on this trip, he wasn't going to make it easy for her. If it hadn't been for Cathy's husband lending her the balance, she wouldn't have been on the plane tonight. *Who knows how I will repay him, but I'll figure it out when I get back. One thing is certain: I'll return every cent to him.*

The drone of the plane makes her drowsy. *These seats are so uncomfortable. Do they really expect one to sleep sitting upright?*

*****

At Frankfort International Airport armed troops escort them to the El Al plane bound for Tel Aviv. Were they informed properly? She was aware of the troubles between Israel and the Syrians, but seriously? Guards on duty to protect passengers in Frankfort? Even though her friends and relatives cautioned her that she was endangering her life, she remained optimistic and confident in God's protection.

Groups go faster through security than individuals, and soon they board their tour bus for their first excursion in Jerusalem. She doesn't know where to look. A cacophony of sounds, smells, and emotions overwhelms her. Who is she to be so fortunate to have the opportunity to experience this? What a pity that she's so unprepared – an immature woman from the south of Africa who thinks she knows something about the Bible. Her claim to be a farmer's wife and the mother of three children wouldn't fly in this country. It's clear from the start of the tour that she would need more time to absorb, develop, understand, and grow. One thing is certain: the woman who'll return home won't be the same as the one who arrived in the Holy Land today.

She quickly learns to look at her experience through different lenses. Traditionally, many places are believed to be authentic and genuine. Sadly, though, churches or other structures were built on these sacred sites. Natural places draw her like the trees, the blue sky, the lakes, and rivers. She can visualise Jesus on a boat on the sea of Galilea or in the setting for the Sermon of the Mount. If it depended on her, she would dismantle all buildings and churches constructed on presumed holy ground.

Who do they think they are? Christians coming here to "bring the gospel" to the unsaved? They are prohibited from discussing their faith with anybody in Israel, but they believe sincerely that their attitude, their caring, their forgiveness, and their kindness will convince non-believers that they have the answer to all society's problems. So, why was she offended by the Arab who yelled at one of the members of their group? 'You Christians! We despise you!'

'What happened? Why is he cursing you?' Alice is baffled. The shopkeeper was friendly and bartered in an amicable fashion while Dora showed interest in the silver bangle. Since she declined to accept his counteroffer, he felt he had the right to insult not only her as a person but all Christians. Alice escapes from the suffocating cave-like shop that smelled like incense and camel sweat. She's been haunted by the encounter for several days. Life is more complicated than she's accustomed to. Her country's troubled history lurks in the back of her mind, but right now she chooses not to dwell on it.

Many individuals from different nations mingle at the conference in Jerusalem. There are Americans, Finns, Canadians, Italians, Germans, Russians, and many more attending. The speakers come from a variety of backgrounds. The speech of Israel's Prime Minister, Menachim Begin, inspires her. This was her first opportunity to listen to a world leader.

Even though this is her first solo trip, she doesn't feel alone. All around her are believers who have come to this place of dying and resurrection. She quickly realises she can't rely on Cathy as a companion.

'But Cathy, why didn't you wait for me? I was looking forward to hearing about the projected exodus of Russian Jews through Finland. You're aware of that, Cathy! How come you left without me? Now I've missed the opportunity.'

Cathy pulls a face and shrugs her shoulders. Alice's tearful rant has no effect on her, and she abandons her promptly to find a seat on the bus. Alice pursues her but turns back when she discovers Cathy has already taken a seat next to a stranger.

She readily meets new people. Their tour guide, Danny, is a Yemenite Jew. Soon, she becomes aware that he's observing her. Maybe he noticed that she was a bit of a loner, doing her own thing. A Bachelor of Arts degree in history is required to work as a tour guide in Israel. Danny has an impressive knowledge of the history, geology, and archaeology of Israel. When the bus stops at a tourist site or they stay over on a kibbutz for the night, he looks for her and they talk.

'Tell me, please. What are you thinking about?' Danny's gaze is piercing and direct.

'I'm trying to process all these incredible impressions. There are things I don't understand that make me feel as if I'm still missing out on so much. For example, why are there so many prisons in your country? I've also noticed that there are armed soldiers everywhere we go. Armed guards accompany school children on field trips. What's it like to live like this? I'm just curious, Danny. I don't expect responses now.'

'Why are you a Christian?' The question takes Alice off guard. Surely, it must be obvious. *Don't the Jews know anything about her religion? that they believe in the same God but believe that the Messiah has already appeared?*

'Would you like the long or short answer? She smiles sweetly at Danny and hopes the other passengers won't notice that she's having a conversation with their tour guide. Never mind, they are all partnered up, and her friend, Cathy, is clearly disinterested in her company or opinion. Maybe this is one of the reasons why she's here today – to share her faith with   Danny. She shares as much as she thinks he'll comprehend, but at the same time she guards herself, trying not to expose too much about her feelings.

As they make their journey to Masada, she takes notes. They'll swim in the Dead Sea today; she won't be wearing her new Gottex bathing suit from the conference in Tel Aviv. That was the one costly purchase she saved for and allowed herself to make. It could be ruined by the concentrated, oily, salty water. It was hilarious to "swim" in a body of water so dense and unrelenting.

'We're going for a walk on the beach after supper. Will you please join us?' Danny notices the hesitation on her face. 'Come on! Everybody is going to bed now.' Torn between duty and pleasure, her eyes follow Cathy as she marches with long strides towards the elevator, they used to take them to their bedroom.

'Thanks for the invitation, Danny. I would have loved to accompany you, but I'm afraid Cathy and the rest of the group will be upset if they see us. I'd hate it if my husband found out I went for a midnight walk on the beach. Can you imagine that? No, goodnight. I'll see you tomorrow at breakfast.'

Like a bean waking up from its dormant phase in damp soil, Alice is torn between what she should do and what she could do. Desperately trying to be true to herself, her joy is repressed by convention.

She's in turmoil the entire journey to the Jordan river. This morning, ten members of their group will be baptised in the river. Her heart implores her to do the same, but she finds herself pushing against a locked gate. Her joy is repressed by convention, though she's desperately trying to be true to herself. The 'what ifs' pile up, and she cowers between the onlookers, shielded by Cathy's lofty structure. *If only I could have been one of them today.*

On the way back to the hotel, she feels sick and disappointed in herself. *Who am I trying to please? What a great opportunity I passed up today because my fear of people outweighed my obedience. Imagine one day telling my grandchildren that I was baptised in the Jordan River. You stupid girl! You're caught up in a small-town community that will soon change in any case.* She's aware that she will be excommunicated from the Dutch Reformed Church once she has been baptised as a believer. Is that why she's such a baby? "Wasn't it enough to have been christened by your parents as an infant?" is what the church fathers would say.

It was time for all the nations to march with the Jews in Jerusalem. This is the largest and oldest march in Israel, with tens of thousands of Israelis and participants from some 90 other countries expected to join. The route to Sacher Park is about ten kilometres long and is laced with crowds of singing, flag-waving jubilant onlookers. She's humbled by the experience of walking under the South African banner, waving a flag in her hand, chanting shalom, hoch shammai (Happy Holiday) and singing Shalom Aleichem. (May peace be unto you.)

Every smiling face, every hand that touched hers with emotion, and every tear that streamed from the face of an onlooker were recorded in her open heart. When she leaves this country tomorrow, she won't associate Jews with shop owners, good tailors, and creators of large families. No, the potpourri of ancient, modern, traditional, war, peace, military, camels, donkeys, traders, tourists, Moslems, Sephardic and Ashkenazi Jews, the wailing wall, and the Al-Aqsa Mosque have multiplied her picture of an ancient land one thousandfold.

*****

It's time to greet them when they arrive in Tel Aviv. Tomorrow they'll be flying home to South Africa, via Frankfort, and from there to Cape Town. It saddens her to say good-bye to Danny and their bus driver. She'll miss his presence, his quiet wisdom, and his knowing looks. He played a huge part in the emergence of her true self – something she desperately needed. Only now does she realise how distorted her image of self is.

Lately, she's been missing her family a lot. Ten days without any contact is a long time, and she tries to picture their excitement at her imminent arrival. Opening their Israeli gifts will be a highlight. She hopes Donald will appreciate the leather belt with the big buckle she chose for him.

After dinner tonight, they'll be entertained by an Israeli dance group before discussing the arrangements for their departure to Ben Gurion Airport. A few people of their tour group have been sick with a tummy bug, and one man is pushed in a wheelchair because he's so weak.

'I'm sorry to inform you that El-Al is on strike, and they won't be able to fly us to Frankfort tomorrow. Alternative arrangements will be made, but one third of the group must remain behind until SAA can arrange a flight for them.' Anxious voices interrupt the speaker. 'What about the sick people? Are their names on your list?' Before he can reply, another voice pipes up. 'I must be on the flight tomorrow. I have important business waiting for me in South Africa.'

One can hear a pin drop while the names of the lucky passengers are read out. 'Susan Jooste, Petro and Kosie van der Merwe, Johanna Albertyn, Cathy Pretorius, Johan, and Annalise Kriel.' She waits with abated breath. What did she expect? Of course, she would be at the bottom of the list. A feeling of despondency wraps itself around her. It feels as if she's the only one left behind. She doesn't know the others in the group very well. Only now does she realise that she'll be practically alone for the next few days. The thought terrifies her, but a new feeling takes hold of her. *This is going to be exciting. I'm going to spend my own vacation on the beach in Tel Aviv. How many other people do I know who are so privileged?*

'Please Cathy, will you do me a favour?' Cathy's suitcase is already packed, and she's ready for an early departure to the Ben Gurion Airport tomorrow morning. 'Sure.

What do you want me to do for you?' Cathy brushes her hair while staring into the mirror.

'Will you please phone Donald as soon as you arrive home and tell him the reason why I'm delayed? I know the children will be terribly disappointed, but what can I do?' She quickly goes to the bathroom so that Cathy won't notice the tears streaming down her face. What's the matter with her? Is she sad because she won't see her family tomorrow evening, or is this feeling of despair because she's missing Danny? If only she could let him know that she was still in Tel Aviv. He is most likely already on his next trip with different tourists. Deep down, she knows that it will take a while for him too to forget about her.

'Sure, Al. I'll give him a call as soon as I arrive. You know, I'm a little envious of you. I wouldn't mind being here on my own for a few days.' Cathy sighs and turns off her bedside lamp. 'I don't think I'm ready to face that empty baby's room yet.'

'Oh, Cathy. I'm so sorry.' Alice is at a loss for words. It saddens her that instead of growing closer during this trip, they have lost their close bond. Will it ever be repaired? She knows she's not to blame, but carrying the terrible burden and possible guilt of what could have or should have happened when Timmy had his accident, must be unbearable. She can only pray that Cathy will find the peace she so desperately needs.

*****

'Where are you from?' Alice dreads this question, as she knows by now that foreigners frown upon white citizens from her country of abode. It's difficult to explain to them that there are legitimate concerns about a 'handover' to most citizens.

117

'I'm from South Africa. I came here to celebrate the Feast of Tabernacles. This is my twelfth day in Israel. I had such a great time. It's hard to believe that it's the Mediterranean Ocean in front of me. What an experience.'

She opens her towel to place it on the rocky beach, a few feet away from the young soldier. He wears his dog tags with pride, and his oiled, tanned skin glimmers in the sun. She can hear the gentle lapping sounds of the turquoise ocean. Oh, bliss. Now she can finally unwind.

The soldier appears to be eager to converse, and she reluctantly turns towards him. She understands she had to let go of her reservations because she wasn't used to the openness of individuals from other countries. *This is how people are. Not shy and withholding, worried that they could be robbed like us in South Africa.*

'I've spent eight years in the army. This war is still a long way from finished. My studies appear to be a waste of time. I studied to become a chartered accountant, but I have hardly spent a year doing my real job.' It feels strange to see so much bitterness and anger in a young person's eyes and face. How would she ever understand what it must be to live in a country where war is a constant threat intruding on everybody's life?

'What work do you do? 'The soldier's glance takes in her figure and Gottex swimming costume.

'I'm a farmers' wife. We live on an export fruit farm.' Alice reaches for the sunscreen in her bag.

'Oh, a farm you say. In South Africa. Would you mind showing me your hands?'

Alice wipes the surplus sunscreen onto her towel and extends her hands.

'May I touch them?' Alice feels embarrassed but can't refuse the strange request. This must be one of the weirdest pick-up lines she's ever heard. She hesitantly offers him her left hand. *What will his next move be?* She wonders.

'What do you do on your farm every day? Your hands are so soft. People who work on our kibbutzim have hard hands. They do all the labour themselves. His sharp gaze makes her wriggle uncomfortably on the beach towel. Nobody has ever been so blunt with her. She's certain now that he isn't a charmer or a smooth talker trying to win her over. What should she say?

'We provide cottages for our paid labourers who live on the farm.' No, that won't make sense to him. He asked her what she does.

She stumbles over her words. 'I do administration work for my husband in our office. I take my children to school every day. But, no, I don't do any hard labour.' Whatever she says now is not comparable to the amount of physical labour these people must do, very often with a gun in their hands.

*****

Lying there on the beach in Tel Aviv in her new Gottex swimming costume, her mind wanders. What happened with her and Cathy's friendship? Why did she desert her and didn't care that she had to stay behind? She thinks of Donald who is their provider and works so hard to be a prosperous farmer even with the handicap of limited funds. For the first time she realises that her parent's ways weren't altogether right or just. It was time to think of her children's future in a different way. If she wanted to live according to her beliefs, she would have to be braver than she had been prepared to be. She wants to kick herself for allowing the fear of people prevent her from

119

being herself. Why didn't she get baptized in the Jordan river? Who are these people who influence her so much?

Feeling sick with disgust at herself, she returns to the safety of the hotel where the other South Africans from her group are staying too. If she had more energy, she could have wandered off to shops or walk along the stunning Mediterranean beach.

Her roommate is sick and the air smells foul from her vomit. The sounds of lively Israeli music cause her stomach to contract. If only she could be out there where the flickering lights attract people like moths to a candle. *If only, what?* She wonders as she falls asleep. They must be at the airport at six o'clock tomorrow morning.

*****

The bus that will take them to Ben Gurion Airport arrives on time. While they drive through the never sleeping city, they sing Shalom Malechim with wary voices. When they arrive at Departures, their tour leader goes to the counter with their passports and return tickets. 'Go to the toilets now. It might be a while before we board the plane.'

'We regret to notify the passengers of flight 738 to Frankfort that it had been cancelled.' Alice can't believe her ears as the announcement is made over the intercom. *Gosh, can't these people settle their differences with their ground personnel and cleaners? No wonder they are always at war with their neighbours. How dare they treat us like this?*

When the subdued party of South Africans return to their opulent hotel on the beachfront, where they'll spend another night courtesy of El Al, they don't feel like singing. Fortunately, she didn't become ill, and she was able to enjoy another day on the beach. She avoided anyone who resembled an Israeli soldier this time.

*****

She finds it difficult to take her gaze away from her lovely young family. Her soft farmer's hands continue to caress them. 'Mom, what did you bring us from Israel?' Donald is happy with his leather belt, which has the inscription "Jerusalem."

Cathy kept her word and called Donald to explain her delayed return. Alice waited in vain for her call to welcome her back or inquire about her stay in Tel Aviv after her earlier departure. To be able to repay her husband, Alice had to work for a year in the neighbouring town.

She swam in her new Gottex swimming costume a lot that summer, enjoying the sumptuous feel of the high-quality fabric. Her speeches about the Feast of Tabernacles at the Women's Christian Society and the local high school, were well received.

The healthy newborn boy Cathy and her husband welcomed nine months later would never be able to replace Timmy, but it must have felt like a miracle to the mourning couple. The vehicle whose tyres brutalised tiny Timmy's body was never found by the detectives.

Alice watched her husband proudly wear his Jerusalem belt; his feet firmly planted on traditional ground. She couldn't help revisiting the Holy Land in her mind while guarding the gates in Jerusalem's wall. Sadly, Alice and Cathy never managed to revive their friendship and the Russian Jews have still not fled persecution through Finland.

*****

Mosaics

It's already dusk when she approaches the mountain pass. Black clouds blown in from the coast and accumulated in the mountain crevices burst open as if on command, and she strains to see the road ahead of her. It will take another hour's drive to get to her destination. If only she could draw the rain curtain back, she'd feel safer.

Her mobile phone rings, and she pulls over to the side of the road. She had a feeling it was Don, and she's relieved to see his phone number on the screen.

'Where are you now?' He seems suspicious and sounds aggressive.

'I'm on my way to Cape Town. Simone scheduled a doctor's appointment for me on Monday. Don, my nerves are shot. I'm struggling to keep going. This way, when you're released from the clinic on Wednesday, we can drive home together.

'Are you crazy, Melanie? What are you thinking? How could you leave our business like this? You need to be there when prospective buyers arrive. You've left me with no choice except to discharge myself from the clinic tomorrow morning.'

Melanie feels how the blood flows from her brain. How is it that Don can't see her logic? Is she the crazy one? 'I've spoken to William, and someone will be on standby to fill in for me. The business won't suffer because we're both out of town for the weekend! Come on! It's not like it's the first time we've both gone away.'

'I'll pick up the car tomorrow morning and drive straight home. Drop the keys off at Simone's place. I don't want to see you.' Don starts yelling, and she moves the phone away from her ear.

'Calm down. Have you completely lost your mind? How am I supposed to get home again? If she can maintain her cool, he may reconsider and become more practical.

'I don't care how you get home again. You should have discussed your plans with me before you left our house and business for a whole weekend.'

'But Don! You weren't contactable. You haven't talked to me in days. How could I have gotten in touch with you? The line is dead on the other end. How rude he has become since she wrote that letter he had to read in front of the other patients! She was tired of pretending and giving him the benefit of the doubt. His behaviour is appalling.

She puts her mobile phone on the passenger's seat and turns on the car's headlights. Her hands are trembling, and tears stream down her cheeks. Checking in her rear mirror to see if any cars are approaching, she joins the stream of cars heading for Cape Town. The windscreen wipers battle to clear the window, and the tyres of the car driving in front of her splash pools of water onto her car's bonnet.

This section of the road is familiar to her. There is a deep crevice on the left side of the road with no safety barrier. If she jerked the steering wheel to the edge of the road, the car would plunge down the mountain. They won't discover her for several days. Nobody would believe she could do something like that on purpose, and they'll believe it was a tragic accident. Her breathing becomes shallow and fast, and despite the cold she feels perspiration streaming from her armpits.

Her hold on the steering wheel is firm, and the tyres refuse to budge. Her eyes are fixed on the furniture truck driving in front of her car. Its logo reads, 'Sunnyside Furniture Removals.' Is it possible? They have used this company's services several times. Like a person reaching for a lifebelt in a stormy ocean, she latches onto this somewhat familiar company.

This isn't the solution to her problems. Even if Don has turned his back on her, there are individuals who care about her.

She'll be safe and sound with her family in an hour.

*****

He waved at her as the bus drove away. The journey from their home to his sister's house in Cape Town where he'd stay for the night, should take six hours. She never imagined sending him on a bus to a luxury rehabilitation centre. Once the bus disappears on the national road, she turns back to enter their office. It'll be strange working without Don. They do everything together. His 'office on wheels', as he calls his car, is standing forlornly next to the pavement in front of their office. It made sense to leave it here rather than keep it locked up and unused in Cape Town. If they see it their clients might not even realise that he isn't there.

She was taken aback when she overheard him telling his hairstylist that he was going to get help for his drinking problem. Wow, that was brave of him to share this news. Being open and honest is presumably part of the treatment and healing process.

The alternative was much worse. She'd already arranged for the removal company to collect her furniture and personal stuff next week. This was going to be the end of their crazy, intoxicated lives. Everything was divided, and she started to pack her portion in boxes. All the sharp knives would have remained with him. After all, he was the cook in the house.

It was almost a relief to cease hoping for things to improve. A person should be aware that autumn has arrived, one should accept it and start to dress warmly. Despite the stubborn faith she still had that one day he'll turn a page, she knew it wasn't destined for her to enjoy a new, sober Don.

The day he realised she didn't bluff and was going south without him; he sobbed and admitted his act was a façade. He dreaded her departure and finally consented to get help at a rehabilitation centre. This was a victory for her. At last, she knows now he loves her more than his favourite white wine. She could see their future in front of them. Perhaps it wasn't going to be an easy road to travel. They'll have struggles, but eventually, they'll be victorious.

Without a doubt she'll be walking right beside him, hand in hand.

*****

Tonight, should be the last night that he ever drinks in the way that only an alcoholic can. She grants him one last evening spent with his family before he enters rehabilitation the next day. The fact that he doesn't call her, doesn't bode well. This is uncommon because they usually talk every day.

Knowing he's spending time with his family and drinking as much as he wants leads her to throw her own pity party. Doesn't he have any understanding of her situation?

Isn't he concerned about her well-being? There aren't many people in this town who know of their situation and whom she may rely on for help. She's going to stay alone for a month while her husband tries to get rid of his demons.

Her thoughts are jumbled. Most evenings after work began cheerfully and amicably, until a few glasses of wine later, she was labelled a whore and a slag.

'What's a slag?' she asked him the following day. 'Why do you ask?' He looks surprised. 'Because that's what you called me last night.' Talk about cognitive dissonance! She had to look up the word in the dictionary.

She develops a voracious appetite for time. The peace and quiet overwhelm her like the fumes of a peace pipe. It scares her to think that it might be taken away from her. These halcyon days are priceless. In the morning she opens the sliding doors of their third-floor bedroom and lies in bed, listening to the ocean take and give, pull, and push, growl, and smile. Candles and baroque music accompany her when she enjoys a hot, slow bath. Finally, she has time to do the things that enrich her, knowing that Don is safe and in good hands.

Rules at the institution are strict, such as no phone calls or visits for the first week. Though she misses him, she's relieved that she doesn't have to listen to his gripes. Knowing him so well, she's convinced that there will be issues. It will be tough not to be able to visit him once he's allowed to since it is a four-hour drive from their home to Cape Town.

'Now you know what it's like to be alone.' Don's mother has no idea what it's like to be alone because one's husband is in a rehab. 'Yes, Pat. I understand you'll always be lonely after your husband's death. It's simply a shame I can't be with Don to encourage him.'

She must step back and let go of her need to be in charge. While he's learning about his new life, she must learn about hers. Fingers crossed after this is over, they'll be able to rejoin their lives again and finally be happy and successful.

*****

'This place isn't as advertised! There are no beach walks, and the front door is guarded. Are you kidding me? The patients aren't allowed to go outside alone.'

It was a huge mistake to have called Don's sister. She hoped to hear some news about Don since she and her husband managed to visit him despite the clinic's strict visitation rules. Even though he wanted to quit smoking, they brought him a large container of cigarettes so that he wouldn't have to suffer. 'Giving up booze is one thing, but smoking helps to soothe his anxieties.'

'Oh, my goodness, Anne. He hasn't smoked for months. Did you discuss this with his councillors? Do you really think it's a good idea for him to smoke again? Melanie is perplexed. How unbelievably stupid. She hasn't been considered; nobody asked for her opinion. It's as if she doesn't exist. Don is safely locked away; he can't escape, he can't drink alcohol, he can't judge her, he can't criticise her, or be a "know it all." People who know about his situation have lots of sympathy. "Poor Don. It must be terrible for him to go through this." They'd say.

It's a good thing she can't speak to him tonight; she'd freak out about his sister giving him cigarettes and ruining his tenuous triumph.

If only she could tell him about their clients today. Even though she had to go above and beyond to fulfil both of their responsibilities, it went extremely well. She hurled herself at her clients with such zeal that a sale resulted. She wished she could make him proud, but he refused to take her call tonight.

Wha the heck! Tonight, she'll celebrate her sale on her own. She turns the CD player on and does a few dance moves to her favourite music. Freedom from the sounds of scraping glass on the counter and gurgling liquid poured into a glass makes her feel liberated. There are no empty bottles to put into black bags – only the sound of her beating heart. This evening, she doesn't have to walk on eggshells, wondering when his mood will change, and she'll change, according to him, into a dreadful, appalling creature. At the very least, she can unwind tonight; nothing awful can happen to her. Nobody will throw wine boxes on the floor; no one will argue with her; nobody is going to kick the furniture or fall into the bath and knock their head, leaving blood splatters on the floor.

Look! This is my kitchen too. I may do whatever I like and go to bed when I'm ready. There's nothing she can do about Don's absence. No amount of worry will change her attitude towards their lives, now or in the future. Her belief that Don will be cured and that they'll have a new future together, free from alcohol and its consequences, causes her to want to laugh aloud.

After dinner, she sits by her computer at the kitchen counter. The psychologist at the clinic requested her to write a letter directed to her husband, not withholding, or beating around the bush. "Say it as it is," were the instructions. It was such irony. Don used to make fun of the "dear Jimmy letters." How would he react to a letter written from the heart, open and honest, telling him exactly how she felt and how his frequent drinking affected her?

There's a good chance he'll despise her after reading this letter. Normally, his blue, begging eyes could melt her heart, but now it feels like he's too far away to hurt her, and she may let go of her reservations. At last, she may express her thoughts and be true to herself.

With trepidation in her heart, she starts to type. "Dear Don. I believe in you, and I'm positive, you'll be cured. I'm waiting for your return and our new life together."

"Please understand that should you begin drinking again, I'll have to leave you. It will break my heart as well as the hearts of everyone who knows and loves us as a couple. Do you realise how serious I am? I can hardly wait to meet the new 'you.' That new person will discover he is gifted and capable of living a complete and fulfilling life without the use of a bottle as a crutch. Above all, never lose your wonderful sense of humour."

Melanie unburdens her heart by following the clinic's advice and directions. Don must recognise that his excessive drinking has a detrimental impact on her.

So, why does she now feel like a deadly snake? Her fangs are spewing venom that has been tainted by horror and evil. Should she feel better now, or was this exercise designed to teach Don something? What will his mother and sister write? Probably only pleasant and reassuring things. Then again, have they got any idea what it's like to live and work with him?

There. I've sent the letter. Will they print it and hand it to him so that he can read it in private?

*****

It's Saturday night. Again. This one is completely different for all the Saturdays they've spent together since they met nine years ago. Today she yearned for the good old days and their usual routine.

129

You're driving me crazy, even more than when we're just going about our daily lives. I contacted you a few times last night, but each call was brief, and your tone was harsh. The second you realised it was me on the other end, your demeanour changed. You went from being polite and nice to nasty and rude. You clearly despise me because I exposed you. Your fellow addicts thought you were a hot shot businessman with a bit of a drinking problem. I swear I had no idea you'd have to read this letter aloud in front of the entire group.

'You stupid woman. How could you? I hate you.' Don's voice sounds harsh and cruel. 'I held up my end of the bargain! You've ruined everything now.'

'Don! Please pay attention to what I'm saying. That wasn't my intention.' The familiar sound of the phone being put back on the receiver, convinces her that he won't listen or attempt to understand her point of view.

What would she have told him if he did listen? There's no point in asking for forgiveness. He has decided it was all her fault and he'd preferably side with his family.

*****

'Mom, take a warm bath and go to bed. I'll call the psychiatrist tomorrow and ask him to prescribe you a sedative and possibly an antidepressant. Pack a case for a few days and leave after work tomorrow. We'll be expecting you.'

'But you don't understand, Simone. I feel desperate. You should see the kitchen. I ripped up all the documents and letters lying on the counter and threw them onto the floor. The house is in a mess. My life is in a shambles. I can't cope anymore. How am I going to drive for four hours in this condition?'

'I understand your confusion, Mom. Simply follow my instructions. Leave after work tomorrow afternoon. You'll be just fine.' Once you're here, we can talk. Do you still have any sleeping tablets? Yes? Well, take one and get into bed now.'

Thank goodness my daughter is a doctor. I'll follow her advice. Three days. I must pack clothes for three days. I'll leave straight from the office. The plants will survive until Don, and I get back on Sunday.

Bliss. As the effect of the sleeping tablet crawls into the dark corridors of her brain, the cold, damp fingers clutching her heart relinquish their steely grip. Sleep is her lover, softly embracing her in its arms.

*****

'What terrible weather to drive in!' We're so glad you're safe, Mom. Come inside; let's talk. Here, give me your case. You must be exhausted.'

Tears well up in Melanie's eyes. She's safe at last. They never have to know about her close shave with death in the pass.

'I have news for you. The doctor wants to see you on Monday, but he's adamant that you should book into the clinic tomorrow morning. They want to start with your treatment as soon as possible. It's critical that you're psychologically and physically strong when you deal with Don's rehabilitation.' Her daughter smells of fresh strawberries. She looks gorgeous in her blue jeans and amber-coloured sweater.

'Do you know what Don is up to? You won't believe it. He wants to leave rehab tomorrow and start work on Monday. I don't know what to do, Simone. This is a recipe for disaster. He's so angry with me about the letter that he won't even have a rational conversation with me.'

131

'We'll take you to the clinic tomorrow, and then he can fetch the car here. We can't stop him, and if he wants to jeopardise his treatment at this critical stage, it's his decision.'

'I can't believe how his mind is working. How long do you anticipate I'll be in the clinic? I only brought clothes for three days.'

'It depends a lot on the medical aid. Don't think about it, Mom. We can lend you clothes or even buy you a few things. Let's take care of you first. Come, follow me. The children have prepared a surprise for you.'

Nicole leads the way towards her bathroom. She smells it first before she notices rose petals strewn across the carpet and bath salts evaporating in clouds of steam enveloping her. Fragrant-smelling candles spread a dim light in the cosy atmosphere. Thick towels are draped on the chair.

'Oh, gosh! This is wonderful! Come here! Let me give you a hug. Her three granddaughters' faces beam with delight. 'Get in, Granny. The water will cool off! Call us if you need help. We'll be in the kitchen.'

When she cradles her head on the rim of the oval-shaped bath, she feels her body relax in the hot water. Who knows what will happen next? But for today, she's safe. Her longing for Don is intense, but she realises she might not see him for a long time, if ever. The grief of his abandonment is deep and sharp, and she ducks her head. Tonight, the love her grandchildren have shown her covers a multitude of sins.

*****

'I'm not in a rush to send you home until you're ready to confront your husband. As I understand it, he discharged himself and has already fallen off the waggon.'

Melanie examines the doctor's expression to see if he's joking. She doesn't think it's a laughing matter. To her, it is one of the most significant failures of her and Don's lives. What a waste of valuable time. The worst insult to her is that he drove past the clinic but didn't stop to see her.

'I'm sure he has learned a lot, and somehow certain processes might have taken place in his mind. My guess is that he can't envision his life without his trusted crutch, alcohol. From now on, we'll concentrate on your next steps, whether they're with your husband or on your own. I'll prescribe medicine to help you, but I would like you to meet with a psychologist daily to guide you towards your growth and possible changes. Not all relationships can transcend an addiction, and we must prepare you for all possibilities.'

'The staff on duty will direct you to the appropriate classes and groups. It will be beneficial for you. The handicrafts are also part of the treatment. Do you have any questions for me?

'What must I make of the fact that Don didn't come to greet me? How do I deal with that?' The doctor hands Melanie a box of tissues. Her tears are close to her eyes. It feels like she's drowning and suffocating at the same time.

'Tell me about your work. Does it work for you if you do everything together? It seems you are very successful as a partnership.' The psychologist has piercing eyes. Melanie knows she can't fool him.

'There are times when I must pull or force him to accomplish his work; nay, it happens frequently. He enjoys sitting by his laptop, waiting for me to tell him what we should do.' The words had fallen out of her mouth. It's not her intention to badmouth her husband. 'He's brilliant at his job, yet he lacks energy and initiative. Despite this, he's clients

133

adore him, and we do very well with the sales. I worry a lot that they will smell alcohol on his breath, though. Don't get me wrong; he doesn't drink during the day or at work. He's also very amusing. I'm certain you'll like him, doctor.'

'I see. What kind of car do you drive? I know it doesn't sound relative, but bear with me.

'I drive a Toyota Corolla, which I love.' *What is the man driving at?*

'And your husband. What does he drive?

'A Fortuner. He claims it's his office, and he must impress his clients.'

'Yes, it is a very nice car,' the doctor concurs. 'Where's it parked overnight?' *Where is he going with this?* She wonders once more.

'His car is parked in the garage, while mine stands outside.' *So, what about it?* She challenges him with her eyes.

'Are you able to see it yet, Melanie? In your relationship, your husband holds the place of honour – in your work, especially, but almost every aspect of your daily life. So, are you surprised that he didn't come to greet you on his way back home? You upstaged him.'

She's stunned. Deep down, she had known this, but she could never verbalise it. Indeed, she needed the services of a professional to point out the realities, the nitty-gritty, and the less-than-appealing issues. Cold and damp fingers throttled her. She feels panicked. What does this information mean? So, what should she do next?

'Right, this is all for today. I'll see you tomorrow at 10 o'clock.' The doctor smiles at her and gets up from his chair to open the door.

*****

'Hello Don. I'm delighted you're picking up the phone. How are you doing? Have you returned to work?'

'Hi Melanie. Yes, I'm back at work. Sorry that the rehab didn't work out for me. I'm afraid I'm drinking again. When will you be back home again? I'm missing you.'

'Oh, Don. I don't know. They said I could stay here until I'm ready to decide. There are some challenging things I need to work out.'

'What do you mean, Melanie? You love me, don't you? I need you here. This is your home, and our work, and our future.' The panic in Don's voice is audible, and she begins to feel terrible for him.

'Of course, Don, I adore you. Maybe I love you too much. The question is, who do you love most? Will it be me or the wine?' She doesn't wait for Don's response. This time, she puts the phone down first.

Why does she have to threaten, justify, and chastise? Everything that had gone before seems wasted and in vain. The energy she requires to beg him once again has been depleted. Her focus is on her recovery. The future without Don seems daunting and almost impossible.

Why not give him another chance and see where it takes them? She draws pictures in her mind of them working together, selling homes, charming clients, depositing money into their bank accounts, and paying off their bond. Didn't somebody recently say: "When I think of Don, I think of Melanie, and vice versa?" Should she draw the line in the sand now while they still have so much love for each other and can toy with the prospect of a great future?

She rushes to the nurse's station due to a panic attack. 'Please, nurse. Help me. I need something to calm me. Look at how my hands are trembling. I was fine until I needed to speak to my husband.' It's important for her that someone understands that she hasn't spoken to her husband for two weeks.

The nurse consults her file and hands her two white tablets. 'Here, take these. It should get you through until tonight's medicine rounds.' Melanie surprises herself by effortlessly taking medication to calm her. Over the last couple of days, she learned that this crutch is the only way she manages to survive these debilitating attacks of fear, panic, despair, and sometimes the urge to end it all.

Her roommate is at a session with her psychiatrist, and their room seems like the only place to go now. She lies down on her bed. The medication is taking its time to take effect, and vivid memories of incidents when Don was intoxicated floods her mind. Her stomach constricts and her throat feels tight, but she can't stop the dark images sticking to her like a spider's nest.

There were many nights he spent sleeping on the couch. There was the time he fell onto his head into the empty bath, the times she found blood all over the house in the morning, the time when he left the car running in the middle of the road in front of their house, the times when she ran around the garden late at night trying to block her ears from his insults. She can't stop these thoughts. When she remembered the night, he locked her into the spare bedroom after she hid his car keys and he called the police, she fled from her bed to go to the recreation room to be with other patients.

'You can stay here as long as you feel you need to recover. Don't feel pressured by Don, your family, or friends. It's your decision to make.' It comforts her to know the doctor isn't judging her.

'What are my options, doctor? Should I return to Don while he's actively drinking, it will just be another car crash. If I don't return, I'll have to fend for myself and start my life all over. I'm not sure if I would know how to do it. I mean, everything is strange and feels daunting.'

'There! You've said it. Indeed. What are your options? Stay in your marriage or leave, and start over again sans your addicted person. Think about it and then we can discuss it further tomorrow at your session.'

Mosaic pieces have a strange way of fitting or repelling. When she sits around the table for her group session, she decorates her flowerpot with colourful pieces of glass. She is completely surprised that she is enjoying the process so much. Her life resembles a pattern in progress. Some pieces fit, while others are a miss-match. Right, wrong, right, wrong. Too many wrongs and it becomes a mess. No, the sides must match. Discard the broken pieces. It won't ever be perfect, but it will sort of make a pleasing, albeit damaged picture.

It will be her decision and she'll have to live with the consequences. In a way, the decision has already been made for her, she's just struggling to picture the completed mosaic. What is missing is the grouting.

*****

This time he answered the phone immediately. She hears a woman's voice in the background. 'Who's on the phone, Don? Whose calling?' the female voice asks.

'Melanie! I'm so happy to hear your voice. When will you be home?'

'It sounds as if you have company, Don. Who is there with you?'

'Oh, its Petro. She's just standing on our bed to move the picture. According to her, its hanging skew. 'Move it more to the left…. No, lift it more. There. That's perfect. Now, get off my bed, you silly woman!'

'So, when can I expect you here, Melanie?'

Another piece of the mosaic fits and slips smoothly into position. Her fingers are sticky from the white glue. The next piece she'll have to shape with her cutting tool. She closes her eyes and runs her fingers over the ragged side of the red tile. Soon, she'll see the result.

'I'll be there at 12 o'clock on Monday morning. Sunnyside Furniture Transport's van should arrive half an hour later. We might finish packing by five o'clock. It will be a long day, but I want to be back in Cape Town by midnight.'

She puts down the receiver, not waiting to listen to Don's protests. Her stride is strong as she walks past the nurse's desk. Today, she won't take any more tablets for anxiety. She wants to complete her mosaic project before she leaves this clinic.

*****

Soul Mandate

'Is that Annachie speaking? I saw your name and number in the real estate section of the weekend newspaper. My name is Richard Ellis. I'm from London, and I'm looking for property to buy here in the Cape Town suburbs. Money is no object – within reason, of course.'

'Yes. This is Annatjie speaking. I would love to help you find the right property.'

Annatjie takes the sandwich she was about to eat from the file labelled "Property for Sale." She scribbles notes on a pad. "Richard Ellis is from London. Wealthy. Haughty English executive."

'Thanks for calling me. What are your requirements?'

'I entertain a lot. My friends from London will visit me often in South Africa. I'll need at least five ensuite bedrooms, large entertainment areas, and an indoor swimming pool with a steam room and a jacuzzi. Do you have something like that for about R10 million? I have been told I should be looking towards that high ground – neighbourhoods called Durbanville or Welgimud or something like that. Please accept my apologies for my poor pronunciation. I didn't realise there were so many Afrikaans speakers here. Are you one of them, too?'

'Yes, but I would describe myself as fully bilingual. One pronounces it as "W e l g e m o e d." Afrikaans is quite a guttural language like Hebrew or Dutch.'

At last! At last. This was the big break I had been waiting for. Sales have been slow during the winter. But now the tide is changing. Silberbauer Properties would be over the moon with me. Just think of the commission on a sale of that size. Be careful now. Don't show your eagerness. Act as if you do this every day.

'I believe I do have the right property for you, Mr. Ellis.' Annatjie must take a deep breath to stay calm. She feels light-headed. Usually, she plans her viewings well in advance. Some estate agents like the surge of adrenaline that comes from unexpected calls like these, but this is out of her comfort zone. Nevertheless, she must gather herself and stay focused.

'I believe I have not one but two properties that should interest you. The one is a Spanish villa with eight bedrooms, a large pool, and it even has its own miniature golf course. It stands on ten acres with beautiful views towards Table Mountain.'

'That's excellent, Annachie. Is it Miss or Mrs?'

'Oh, don't bother about the formalities. Just call me Annatjie.' *There is no reason for clients to know anything about my private life.* 'The other house has six bedrooms, beautifully appointed with a tennis court and sprawling lawns. The villa is on the market for R12 million, but they will look at offers. The one with the tennis court is on the market for R8 million. Do you want to view these properties?'

'Sure. I'd like to see both. It's just ten o'clock. Could we meet at noon? Unfortunately, I don't have a car available; I'm staying at the Radison Hotel. How will I get to you, or could we meet here?'

'I could fetch you with my car, Mr. Ellis. No problem. What is your room number?'

'It's 1023. I'll be waiting for you in my room. Thanks, my girl.'

'I'll phone the owners to make sure they can accommodate us this afternoon. Bye. See you later.'

This could be the first big one. I better be good today. At Silberbauer Property's monthly reward meeting, they put a lot of emphasis on the appearance of their estate agent's appearance. They keep telling us that looking good is part of selling.'

She checked her make-up in her hand mirror. Maybe she shouldn't wear the slacks. No, her new short Polo skirt will be more appropriate. Her legs are still a little white from the winter and a lack of sun, but with her new stylish shoes, she knows she can pull it off. *I don't look bad at all, check that figure too.*

*****

The Radisson Hotel is one of Cape Town's most prestigious hotels. It is situated close to Cape Town's popular Alfred and Victoria Waterfront. Would Mr. Ellis be coming from old or new money? Her guess is that it is new money, as her other clients who came from the aristocracy, would stay at the Mount Nelson, a Belmond Hotel near the Gardens in Cape Town. The Radisson is a few metres off the shoreline and looks across the waters toward Robben Island, where Nelson Mandela was incarcerated.

*****

'Come to my room.' Richard said in reply to Annatjie's desk call. He hurriedly went to the bathroom, patted his cheeks with his Armani after-shave, and took a few quick squirts of breath deodorant. A quick glance into the mirror confirmed his thoughts about himself – he still fancied himself with the ladies. And why not? With his credit rating and his more than generous expense account and salary, he was a good catch, even if he had to say it himself. He felt exuberant knowing that Annatjie would be with him soon.

She knocked softly on the half-open door to room 1023. Despite feeling a tremor of anticipation run through her, she's confident that she's doing the right thing.

'Go the extra mile. Meet your clients at the airport. Take them out for lunch. Be better in every way than your competitors.' Silberbauer Properties has a reputation for outstanding service and she's proud of their achievements. If she can clinch a deal today, she'll qualify for the conference held in Mauritius in December.

Ellis was taken aback by Annatjie's appearance. She flashed him a quick, wide smile, while her big, almond-shaped brown eyes sparkled too. Instantly, he knew that Annatjie, with her svelte figure, would be his. He has seduced many beautiful women on his 'business trips.' Working for the multinational Megabyte Insurance Corporation had many perks. The company was famed for its global ability to attract billions of dollars of clients' investments. But the negative side of their fame was for the legal cases against them for non-payment of claims and never losing since their lawyers literally ran the global legal system.

He sneered at the old saying, 'Don't mix business with pleasure." Why can't he have both? He used his wealth almost exclusively for pleasure. Beautiful women like Annatjie, combined with the thrill of buying an exclusive property, was the perfect cocktail for a successful man like him.

Sure, he'd buy a house from her. She would get her commission from Silberbauer after the registration of the property in his name, but he would give her a wad of dollars after he'd seen the properties. He had already decided that he'll give her thirty one-hundred dollar bills after she brought him back to the hotel, and they had celebrated the sale with champagne and oysters in his suite, where they will draw up the preliminary.

'How can life be so good?' thought Ellis. He licked his lips in anticipation. The girl he met in Miami last week didn't have the class this one has. No, she was quite demanding and nothing special.

He adapted what he believed to be his young and carefree manner and gestured to Annatjie to step into his suite.

*****

She paused at the door, taking in the opulence of the luxurious suite. It was clear that he had access to money aplenty. He wore a London-tailored Saville Row suit, soft calf-leather Italian shoes, and an expensive but overwhelming musk after-shave. A huge bouquet of proteas dominated the round table in the corner of the room.

As he took her hand in his, he gave her a shiny smile. His hand felt flabby and a bit greasy, like a dying fish taking a desperate breath through its quills. She hopes he didn't notice that she surreptitiously put her hand on her hip, where she wiped it against her skirt. It was impossible not to note the artificial fragrance on his breath as he stood close to her, invading her space in the manner of a lover or a confidante. Annatjie knew he would never be either of them.

'Hello. Thank you very much for fetching me. Please take a seat so that I can give you some background. I have all day and the evening too. I hope you are free?'

She ignores his comment and takes a seat in one of the low but comfortable easy chairs. He remained standing. She noticed he took an overlong look at her legs as she crossed them. Ellis was reminded for a split second of Sharon Stone crossing her legs in the movie Basic Instinct. The fact that her well-formed legs were those of an athlete made him feel good. 'I'd like to show her off to my friends.' He thinks.

'Yes, I'm in the market for a few properties in South Africa. My company has instructed me to buy several houses – two here in Cape Town in a good area and a few in Johannesburg. Did you manage to arrange access for today? If not, I'll be free tomorrow too.'

Mm mm. Let's see. I'm not sure if I would like to travel to fetch you again tomorrow. 'I managed to arrange access to two properties. Unfortunately, the villa's owners are abroad, and they didn't leave a key. I'm certain you will love both the other properties.'

Annatjie was well-versed in all the signs and portents given by clients. She has studied the significance of body language for the sales process – the way a client would stand, whether the husband or the wife was the decision-maker, the protective folding of the arms across the body, and the moment when it was all over when the wife took her handbag.

In Ellis, she noted a few red flags, but she hadn't sold anything for several months, and since estate agents don't get paid a monthly salary, she was under unbearable pressure with the heavy debts and commitments of her mortgage, car payments, insurance, and other liabilities. Come what may, she needed this sale, and if Ellis was the way to go, she'd just have to close her eyes, switch off her senses, and get the sale signed up. Anything to get the coming ordeal over with. She gritted her teeth and hoped it looked like a smile. She'll try her best to ignore the way he sits to assert himself, with angular crossed legs, touching the side of his nose like a person who deals with big money, but with extreme caution.

Come hell or high water, this deal just had to come right, even if she was going to hate every moment.

'The funds are all available through a bank draft. To prove our credibility, we're prepared to pay the full amount on signature.'

'That doesn't work like that in our country. A deposit will suffice, and the balance will be paid on transfer.' Annatjie wonders if this isn't a huge money-laundering racket, but there is no point in rushing ahead yet. She first must show him the properties and see if he is prepared to put pen to paper. '

Ellis is impressed with Annatjie's knowledge and professionalism. So, she's not a dumb blonde after all. He wonders if she'll guess what his real intentions are.

A knock on the door made her jump. She felt how the car key she held in her hand pressed into her skin. Ellis moved his bulk towards the door. She noted the wide-legged gait of a man whose upper thighs wouldn't allow his legs to come together.

'Ah! Thank you very much'. A chamber maid steps inside, pushing a trolley with cups and coffee. 'Will you please pour us coffee, Annachie?' Annatjie decided to ignore the mispronunciation of her name. She knows the "tj" sound was difficult to pronounce for English people. 'Sure. Do you take milk, Mr. Ellis?' *The man is very thorough; there are even croissants with the coffee.*

'Yes, thank you. I would like milk in my coffee. What wine do you like? Red or white?

'Annatjie pretends not to have heard. 'Now, Mr. Ellis, what would you like to see first? I brought you brochures with the details of the two houses. Here, have a look.' Annatjie hands him a file she prepared before she left the office an hour ago. Her colleagues know where she was and should they not hear from her within the next hour, someone will call her on her mobile phone to check on her.

Richard smiled and glanced quickly at Annatjie's legs as she uncrossed them. 'I'm in your hands completely. You'll have to show me. As I said, I have the whole day. And the night.' He giggled nervously, admonishing himself for revealing his hand too soon.

'Right, let's go. Thank you for the coffee and croissant. I needed that. I'll take you to one of our show houses in Welgemoed. Then, we'll look at some of those in the upper price range. I'm convinced I'll have something you'll like.' After the words slipped out, she regretted saying that.

'You certainly do, Annachie!' Ellis smirked, enjoying the innuendo. He thought maybe she did too, but he wasn't certain. He was already relishing what he had planned for later. Somehow, he must find out if she has somebody waiting for her at her home. For now, she seems unattached and very businesslike.

*****

He noted the way she drove. She displayed all the signs of an efficient driver: arms extended, the car seat pushed well back, rally-style, crisply, and attentively. His guess was that she was an introvert, but despite her reticence to wow or flatter her clients, she overcompensates with her intellect.

Driving to the suburbs now, she changes from an estate agent to a tour guide. 'Have you been to the top of Table Mountain yet, Mr. Ellis?'

'Please call me Richard. Enough of all the formalities. No, I haven't. Would you accompany me? Please, go with me.' Annatjie throws her head back and laughs, dismissing his request.

Too soon, to his liking they pull up in front of an American-style four-bedroom home. There is a "Sole Mandate" sign from Silberbauer at the entrance. Richard doesn't need to know how hard she fought to get that mandate for her company. The driveway embraces a sprawling lawn where a fountain creates a mini roundabout. The place is impressive, and she's sure Richard will agree.

She unlocks the door before she steps aside for Richard to enter the house through the double doors ahead of her.

'Please excuse me. I need to deactivate the alarm. As you know, that is imperative to have in South Africa.'

Ellis did a quick inspection, noting the high standard of engineering. Annatjie doesn't comment but marvels at the different way men and women look at properties. The structure, the standard of workmanship, the heavy gold-plated bathroom fittings, the position of the sun, the security, and the size of the pool concern male buyers. Women notice wardrobes, the lay out of the kitchen, and the quality of the bathrooms. Since Richard is looking to impress his friends, she doesn't expect him to investigate in too much detail.

'I like space. A place needs to be big for me to be happy. Ellis's accent had elements of the Hammersmith London accent mixed with the pseudo-Manhattan nasal twang that some English executives like to imagine makes them sound successful. Annatjie noticed that his accent slipped now and then, as if he wasn't sure who he really wanted to be. Still, the man seemed to mean business. After all, that was what she wanted. She kept telling herself to stay focused – to get this one over with. She shouldn't overthink everything, like it is her habit to do. While keeping her cards close to her chest, he still knows nothing about her; she's learning more about him.

Clinching a deal is a bit like a love affair, she muses. The advertising, the response, the meetings, the dialogue, the measuring up of what is on offer, which costs, which caveats, then the display and the viewing, the excitement, and the climax. There is also the possibility of competition of another estate agent – the walking away, the empty show house, and the turning off the lights, putting on the burglar alarm, and then going home to the hollowness and the abyss.

But, with Ellis, this wasn't a love affair. This time, Annatjie is convinced that she will do the hit. She would get the deal and the commission.

'Right, Richard, 'she said brightly. Let's look at a house I know you'll like. It's not far from here. It was originally built for the Taiwanese government. They aren't taking it now. The price is very reasonable, at R8 million. There are six double bedrooms, all ensuite. The reception area is massive, with a large lounge, a games room, a library, and a study. There are three remote-controlled garages, a pool set in five acres of garden, and good security. If you are interested in the new designer furniture, it can be included. Would you like to view it?

'Sure. Let's go then.'

Wow, this girl understands me well, thinks Richard. He couldn't resist the temptation to slap Annatjie's left thigh. She flinched and gave him a quick, forced smile.

What must one do to earn one's money nowadays? And why must all the available money be in the hands of people like this? Where are the good ones to keep and hold us? She puts her car in gear and pushes the engine hard. In her rear-view mirror, she watches the security gates close behind her car. *One down, one more to go.*

*****

Mariki Kriel

About the Author

An Eye-opener and other short stories
Mariki Kriel

The creator of **An Eye-opener and other short stories** goes by the pen name **Mariki Kriel**. She is a poet, and writer who self-published **Au Pair Extraordinaire, Rapid Heartbeats** and **Die Vol Vrou (Mariki Lavelle)** on Amazon.

She is a mother, grandmother, real estate agent, qualified carer, businesswoman, artist, poet, and writer. She writes about her life experiences as an au-pair and live-in carer during COVID-19 in the UK with great understanding.

Her objective is to find meaning in the difficulties she faces as an older single woman striving to make it. She has a degree in Psychology and Afrikaans-Dutch and has several certificates in real estate and caring.

She relocated to the UK after 28 years of success as an estate agent, where she was informed during job interviews that she lacked "area knowledge."

After ten years working in the UK, Mariki recently moved back to her native South Africa. She strives to balance her passions for reading, writing, painting, socialising, soaking up the sun, and spending time with her 12 talented grandchildren with the rest of her responsibilities.

Her keen interest in people and their behaviour, motivates her to continuously improve herself. She has finally mastered the ability to enjoy her own company.

Printed in Great Britain
by Amazon

37017436R00086